The envelope was marked
SPECIAL DELIVERY

Inside was a single sheet of paper, and pasted to it were letters cut from newspapers and magazines. There was no salutation.

"Stop the movie or die."

Underneath was the signature. An octagon with a cross inside and two crossed shepherds' staffs behind it —the symbol of the Flock of God cult.

My two big investments—the movies and hydroponics—had been singled out for destruction. The power of God as represented here on Earth by the Reverend Smith had promised to blow the financial future of Billy Nevers all to Hell.

FAST MONEY SHOOTS FROM THE HIP

by

Joseph Mark Glazner

WARNER BOOKS

A Warner Communications Company

Warner Books are
distributed in the
United Kingdom by

HAMLYN PAPERBACKS

WARNER BOOKS EDITION

ISBN: 0-446-90164-4

Cover design by Gene Light

Cover photo by Jerry West

Warner Books, Inc., 75 Rockefeller Plaza, New York, N.Y. 10019

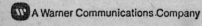 A Warner Communications Company

Printed in the United States of America

First Printing: March, 1980

10 9 8 7 6 5 4 3 2

To Louis and Sophie
who met at the movies in 1925

Chapter One

It was well past three in the morning when Clem Dunkin called. He insisted it was important. It couldn't wait, and he couldn't tell me over the telephone.

Now, I like Dunkin, but not at three in the morning. Not when I have to crawl out of a nice warm bed so soon after I'd crawled in.

Dunkin was a little too dramatic at times. Even for an actor. And a practical joker, too.

I got up, put on some clothes, and moved out to the sitting room so I wouldn't wake her. She was sleeping so soundly she hadn't even heard the telephone. I wish I hadn't either. I envy those people who can sleep through anything.

From where Dunkin said he was calling from, it should have taken five minutes to walk. I told him which door to use so he'd be able to come right up without running into the night clerk. Not that I had any ulterior motive sneaking Dunkin past Moe at the desk. But I have this rule. The fewer people who know my business, the better.

Dunkin showed up seven minutes later and announced himself by a light tap on the door.

"It's open, come in," I said, pouring myself a drink. That was the last thing I needed. My stomach felt like a closet full of rusty coat hangers.

The door opened. I dropped some ice into my glass and poured a fist of Glenlivet. Dunkin came in with a

7

smile on his face. Not a smile, in hindsight, but more a smirk.

He didn't walk in either. He kind of slid in, holding the door handle with his left hand and his stomach with his right. His left hand let go of the door handle and grabbed for the back of the Morris chair. He straightened up and stared at me stiffly, his lips tight, his nostrils flared.

I could see it coming. He was going to do James Cagney at the end of that film where George Raft gets Cagney with a machine gun and the girl with a couple of smooth lines.

"Okay, Dunkin," I said, "what's on your mind?"

I tried to sound angry but I was too grogged to sound anything. He didn't seem to care either way.

He was still holding his stomach like he'd been shot, only he had on a white shirt underneath his jacket and there wasn't any blood.

Moving his arm along the back of the Morris chair, he took a wobbly step toward me with all the exaggerated slowness of a drunk, which I knew he wasn't because I'd just spoken to him a few minutes before and he didn't sound drunk.

"Cagney," I said. "Right?"

Thinking maybe if I humored him he'd go away.

But no, he just shook his head. I had this feeling it was going to be a very long night. I took a long slug from my glass and emptied it.

"You want something to drink, Dunkin?" I asked, holding up the second glass.

He took another step forward and stammered, "Ten thousand . . ."

I waited but he seemed to be stumbling with the words.

"Tehhh . . ." he muttered, then sank to the floor.

It bothered me the way he hit the rug on his knees. I'd seen Dunkin take worse pratfalls than that. He'd do anything to get a reaction if he thought you weren't paying attention. But there was something about this particular fall that set me off.

"Dunkin, are you all right?" I asked, coming toward him.

I was too late. He pitched straight forward, his face smashing against the edge of the coffee table, sliding off and coming to rest flat on the floor. Then I saw it.

The back of his jacket was dark with blood. A black hole big enough to fit two fingers stared up at me from the middle of his back like an evil eye.

I wanted to believe it was some kind of joke; that it was all being done with mirrors. But it wasn't.

I called an ambulance and the police in that order. While I waited, I kept a cloth pressed to the wound. I already knew it was too late though. He'd been dead when he'd walked through my door.

This was no accident. Dunkin had been on his way to tell me something. Important. I racked my brain. Ten thousand. Ten thousand what? How did it all fit together? How did I fit in? There was no question in my mind that I was in over my eyeballs. But how and why?

But I'm getting too far ahead of my story.

First, my name's Billy Nevers. I live in the Ritz Hotel downtown because I can afford it now and because I don't like making beds. I'm not rich. You don't make real money handling other people's money unless you're a bank. Leastways I don't. I work for a living just like you. Only you probably think what I do sounds strange. Maybe it is, but it's a living.

There's a thousand things I'd rather be doing than work, but most of them cost money. The one good one that doesn't takes a lot of time, patience, and just the right person. Sometimes that happens and it's nice. In between, I take care of business.

I won't do just anything for money. But what I will do has to be for a lot, and it's got to be legal. Maybe you think there wouldn't be a lot of people running around giving out that kind of work. There aren't. When there is one, there's usually a catch. I try to weed out the bad from the good. But sometimes you don't really know the score until you're halfway through the game. Besides, sometimes it's just a show of good faith in humanity to give the other guy the benefit of the doubt.

I grew up in a part of town where hubcaps were legal tender. I got thrown out of school for the last time when I was sixteen for hitting the principal. If old man Pender, head messenger for Winston's Securities on Bay Street, hadn't given me a break and hired me as a runner, I might have stayed bad the rest of my life. If Mr. Winston himself hadn't taken an interest when I wanted to study for my license, and if he hadn't gotten some of the formalities over my education waved, I might still be running stocks and bonds up the back stairwells of Bay Street. In the end, you have to make your own points, but you have to get somebody to let you in that first game so you can show them how you play.

One thing I learned about the money game a long time ago—there's more ways to make money than there are to get cancer. And even more ways to lose it.

I've done both. I know firsthand the toughest part is holding on to what you got. I'm not particularly lucky with my own money. I don't usually keep what I make very long. But I have a knack for coming out on the winning side when I handle other people's money. So that's what I do.

Word gets around. I don't advertise or even have a listed number. Somehow, people find me. Maybe we all attract like types. Mine are usually stray dogs with peculiar problems.

It's not glamorous maybe, but it's a living, and it's mostly clean.

If it's so clean, you ask, then how come I ended up on the receiving end of a dead body?

Chapter Two

It all started six weeks before. It seemed like a lifetime ago.

It was one of those periods in my life when things were all falling into place. I had the tax people off my back. I knew I wasn't finished with them, but I figured I'd bought enough time to make more than they'd be able to grab off with their teeth-sharpened pencils. I was putting all my energies into getting a little ahead.

A deal I'd put together a while back was about to bear fruit. Actually vegetables. Hydroponically grown vegetables. I'd put the money together to finance construction of a full-scale commercial production factory to grow vegetables without soil.

For my troubles, I got a hundred thousand in cash for finding the money and a big piece of the action during the first profitable year of production. The action looked okay. The entire production had already been bought up by Anglo-American Limited, one of the largest grocery wholesalers in North America. I stood to take in two hundred thousand dollars from the transaction during the coming year, on top of the hundred thou.

Ten years ago, three hundred thousand dollars would have represented a nice piece of change. Now it's a second-rate prize in the monthly lottery. You can be damned sure if they're giving that much away for box tops and candy wrappers, it ain't worth much.

On top of that, I was looking at sharing the better

11

half with the tax people unless I got smart. I was in the market for a tax shelter.

I had gone to Greenwood to watch the ponies. I don't usually bet the ponies, but I like to watch them run. It's a good excuse to be outside. I'd gone down to the fence and was leaning up against a light pole watching Jenny Gay run the legs off of favorite Kitchen Sink. While I watched, I mulled over my fortunes and tried to figure how to make them better. I find I do my best thinking when I'm concentrating on two things at once.

Three things at once I'm not good at. I didn't hear him come up. I didn't hear him calling my name, and when I felt someone slapping me on the back, I thought I was being mugged. I spun around with my fists cocked to find Lazlo Pope staring at me somewhat bewildered, with his palms out flat toward me. If I didn't know him, I probably would have taken a swing. He is remarkably ugly. Dark and hairy with a bald spot dead center in the middle of his head and a black ring of greasy curls running around it like the type of halo that you'd imagine the devil might grow. I knew him all right. If I didn't, I guess he wouldn't have been slapping me on the back.

"Jesus, Pope, you scared the crap out of me," I said, lowering my fists and holding my hand out to shake his.

He hesitated, then pumped my hand vigorously. Pope was about my size, but he had an iron grip and the strength in his hands of a man twice his size. He once told me he'd worked for two years in his native Hungary wringing chicken necks in a meat packing plant.

"Did you have money on this one?" he asked, pointing back toward the finish line. I looked over just in time to see Kitchen Sink nose out Jenny Gay at the wire.

"I just come to watch," I told him.

"Me, too." Pope slapped my back again. "The smell of horseshit makes me nostalgic for the Old Country. I come here, take a few deep breaths, and remind myself I'm better off not going home."

Pope laughed heartily. It was an old joke with him.

12

Besides being a full-time chicken killer in the Old Country, he'd been a part-time troublemaker. The Soviets came in in 1956 and started locking up whoever they could get their hands on. Lazlo Pope was on their list, but they didn't get him. He escaped, made his way to Berlin, then to Toronto as a teenage refugee. He tried getting work as a chicken plucker, but there wasn't any. He ended up as a driver for the Canadian Broadcasting Corporation, which had become a magnet for the Hungarians who had fled. He learned to speak English with the same imitation BBC accent that most Canadian broadcasters affected back when English Canadians still thought the British were superior stuff.

Pope had a knack for being in the right place at the right time. He kept hanging around the shows and the show people and started writing scripts on speculation. He finally sold some and wormed his way into directing at the television network. In those days, the golden boys of Canadian television had a first-class ticket to Hollywood if they could get a U.S. green card, which allowed you to work. Pope did. He went off to Hollywood and directed a number of financially successful but mediocre films. Then came a string of bad luck with five bombs in a row, and Pope couldn't get himself arrested in the City of Angels.

Five years before, he'd returned to Canada. There was a lot of hoopla about his homecoming in the press, but not much else. He did two low-budget sex films that paid the rent on his apartment and the monthly on his car. He did TV episodes and commercials to make ends meet. In a word, he was surviving until he'd get another chance at the brass ring—that one commercial success that would make everything all right again.

I knew all this because we once had a mutual friend, a showgirl named Peachie Cain. Peachie had introduced me to all the Hollywood types in Toronto. She'd done the circuit—Rome, Paris, New York, Vegas, L.A.—picking up gigs on the chorus line in dinner clubs and bit parts in four dozen pictures before she'd packed it in and come home.

She used to assure me that making films in Hollywood was no different than Toronto or, for that matter, anywhere else.

"The decimal point's a little farther over in Hollywood," she'd say. "But the people are the same. A world full of five-foot-four men and six-foot-two women. That's why nobody in movieland ever stays married. Not enough kissing on the lips."

She used to laugh a lot before she started hanging around a bad, fast crowd and got herself killed. But that's another story.

Pope had approached me with a film deal earlier in the year when I was getting the money together for the hydroponics deal. Investing in films in Canada can be a good move tax-wise if you have the money to lose. If the deal is set up right, you can deduct as much as two and a half to five times what you invest from your income taxes. It's a nice legal tax shelter. A tax shelter's a little like being able to deduct a hundred kids on your tax returns but not having to feed them. But tax shelters are only good if you have some income to deduct from. At that time, my cash flow was a slow dribble. Even if I had the money, I didn't like the sound of the deal. I wasn't in a very knowledgeable position to judge Pope's ability to direct. Pope sounded like he knew what he was talking about on that side. But he was riding two horses. He was also trying to raise the money. When he talked about the financing, nothing smelled right. At least, not to me. The numbers didn't make sense. Every time I asked about the budget, he'd want to talk costumes or sets. On top of that, he chain-smoked machine-rolled marijuana and kept saying, "That's cool," whenever I said he didn't look like he'd really worked on the numbers.

Now I got nothing against people smoking grass or anything else. But not when they're asking me for money. Maybe it's just a backwash of my conservative cold-climate upbringing, but I like my bankers to think numbers are something you keep in your books, not something you smoke.

When he first approached me, I explained my

14

financial position. Even if I wanted to, which I didn't, I couldn't, because I didn't have the money to invest. I gave him a couple of people I knew who might be interested in investing, but I warned him he'd have to straighten out his bookkeeping before anyone took him seriously.

That was the last I'd heard from him until he'd slapped me on the back halfway through the ninth.

He had a certain easiness that said things were going right for him. They were. He told me he'd knocked around for two months after I'd last seen him trying to raise the money, but no one would touch him. Then, he had a stroke of real luck. He'd had his project picked up by a producer. A real pro who'd raised the money and was ready to go into production.

Pope had satisfaction written all over his big-nosed face. He kept slapping me on the back and asking how things were going for me. But before I got a chance to answer, he'd run off at a mad chatter about how things were going for him. I didn't mind. I was interested in the deal. From what I could gather from Pope, the deal sounded like it had shaped into just the kind of tax shelter I'd been looking for. Pope's producer had structured the financing like a stock market offering. Enough points had been sold to cover production, but there were still a few small blocks of stock available.

I told Pope I was interested in hearing more. He said he was meeting his producer later that night for drinks at the Lazy Susan and invited me to join him. I said I would.

It seemed like an innocent enough meeting. Two high rollers with a run of luck, crossing paths at the same time. It was the kind of coincidence that made bad theater.

Chapter Three

The Lazy Susan is a midtown bar off Avenue Road about a mile and a half from the Ritz. The weather had gone sour. The streets were still clean, but the wind had an ugly sting to it. I decided to walk just the same. I'd been getting too car-lazy and was starting to feel like a pig looks.

I'd been renting a car for the past several months—one of those Plymouths that looks like a Chevy. I don't like cars in general, but I needed this one to run back and forth to the hydroponics plant. We'd located the plant near Ajax on a strip of unfarmable land. I fought the traffic a half dozen times a week to go out there.

I walked up Avenue Road toward the Lazy Susan. I was enjoying the fact that I was able to walk faster than the traffic jams. But I wasn't enjoying the cold. By the time I reached the bar, my nose was cherry-red and my ears were about to drop off.

The Lazy Susan is a multilevel bar. The ground floor is mostly disco dance floor and standup bar where the meat market crowd hangs out. Upstairs is Art Nouveau neo-African—lots of palms, deck chairs, long-legged cutesy models and other beautiful people.

I found Pope upstairs. He was sitting with two very attractive women. I recognized Catherine St. Catherine. After Genevieve Bujold, Catherine St. Catherine was probably Canada's best-known international film star. I'm not a follower of movieland, but I'd picked up the odd pieces of her story. She'd had three very

16

successful pictures in Hollywood. Then like Pope, she had a run of turkeys. Word went out that she was a Jonah, and no one would touch her with a barge pole. She'd come back to Canada three years before and had been doing guest appearances on quiz shows. She was heavily involved with Pope and, at one time, was living with him. I knew that because they both made front page not too long ago. She'd emptied a pistol at him during a domestic squabble. When the police arrived, they were still going at it with bare knuckles and had smashed every piece of furniture, dish, and window in the apartment.

I met Pope after that incident. He was living alone at the time.

From the way they were carrying on at the Lazy Susan, they had kissed and made up. I was only half right.

Pope introduced me to Catherine first. She was more striking in person than she was at ten feet on the big screen. She's one of those rare women who can wear her hair dyed platinum blond and not look cheap. She looked like an intelligent version of Marilyn Monroe. Pope introduced her as the star of his next picture.

The second woman was as striking but in a very different way. More handsome than pretty. Tailored tweed rather than silk frills, but still very feminine. Her name was Danielle Davis. Dani for short. She was Catherine St. Catherine's roommate.

"You don't have to be lesbians to live together," Catherine laughed, breaking the ice immediately. She grabbed my arm and pulled me down into the seat between Dani and herself. I was facing Pope across the glass-top table. It gave me an embarrassingly close view of Catherine St. Catherine's other hand under the table playing piano tunes on Pope's upper left thigh.

Pope and Catherine were both drunk and foul. Pope pointed to me and talked as if I weren't there.

"Billy Nevers's the guy who made his first million before he was twenty-two buying and selling pork belly futures."

"Pork bellies?" Catherine eyed Pope suspiciously, then gave me the once-over.

"Bacon," Pope explained. "Billy's the original capitalist pig."

"Male chauvinist too, right?" Catherine tried running the pun into the ground. The alcoholic stench on her breath was strong enough to remove paint from five feet away.

I guess I was already beginning to show my impatience.

"We're just kidding you, Billy-boy," Pope said. "Isn't that right, girls?" ·

Dani looked down in her drink and didn't say a word. The other one should have been so smart.

"Maybe you're kidding, but I'm not." Catherine spoke to Pope in a slurred voice.

"I thought I was going to meet your producer," I said, making no attempt to hide my irritation.

"Relax," Pope replied as he got up, nudging Catherine to join him. He nodded in the direction of Dani. "You got nice company. What's the rush?"

It came out "Whad's dhe rush . . ." Drunk was the only time Pope's perfect CBC imitation BBC accent slipped its moorings and reverted back to the Old Country.

"Led's go dancing," he said, dragging Catherine toward the disco below, leaving me alone with Dani.

My idea of a good time isn't sitting around saloons while a couple of drunks run you into the ground. On the other hand, Pope was right about the company. Dani was a doll.

"I apologize for Catherine," she told me in between sips of Perrier. "She's only like this when she gets drunk."

"I hope it isn't too often," I said.

"She and Pope are celebrating. This movie means so much to her. If you've ever been down . . ." She didn't finish the sentence, but I knew what she meant firsthand. I'd been drunk a few times in my life, too.

"Okay." I nodded. "I understand. Now, what about you? What do you do?"

She laughed at my flat-footed approach. It was a nice hearty laugh and one that told me she wasn't put off by my bad manners.

"I do a number of things," she told me, then listed a little acting, a little singing, a little dancing, a little set designing, a little special effects. She'd managed to survive in the gray area of show business between making it and not making it for the better part of a dozen years.

"It's all a matter of luck." She shrugged. "The question is whether or not you've got the energy to hang in until your time comes."

The nice thing about her was that she wasn't bitter or cynical. She accepted what was, and tried to make the best of it, or at least, chose the better of two bad situations.

"There are three kinds of people in the world," she said. "Winners, losers, and survivors. The survivors are the ones who just about break even. They go home sometimes with a little less in their pockets, but it doesn't ever kill their dreams."

She had a nice way of putting things, and I couldn't help liking her. When she started asking me about what I did, there wasn't any saucer-eyed greed or demure lip-licking when we talked dollars and cents. She made me feel like a regular human being, not like a used cash register.

"Lazlo said you made your first million before you were twenty-two."

"Actually, two point three million in six months," I corrected her, then added, "and it took me three more months to lose it."

She laughed. In the right spots. I told her about the hydroponics plant. She told me how she'd grown up in the country and had her own tomato patch.

"What's your interest in the film business?" she asked.

"Just exploring the possibilities," I told her, being purposefully vague. I wasn't sure myself what I was doing, or if I really was in. I was too vague for this one.

"It's an expensive way to get laid," she warned.

It was my turn to laugh.

"No, I don't suppose you're that type," she laughed, too.

Just then Pope came back. Alone. He informed us that Catherine was in the ladies room throwing up.

Dani excused herself and went off to look after her friend.

Pope sat down heavily.

"She always gets sick when she drinks too much," he said flatly.

I nodded.

"We were having a good time, right?" he asked with a wave of his hand.

I just sat and stared at him. He was too drunk to insult.

"You know something, Billy, I really love that woman. She means more to me than anything else in the world."

He was starting to get sloppy. I changed the subject

"Is this producer friend of yours going to show?" I asked.

Pope shook his head, no. He'd called him right after Catherine had gone to look at the toilet bowl. The producer was tied up in a late-night meeting. He sent his apologies and asked Pope to give me a copy of the prospectus. Pope pulled one out of his briefcase and handed it to me.

I took it and the producer's number and promised to call if I was interested. Then I asked if there was anything I could do for Catherine. He shook his head no, apologized for a lousy time, and ordered another drink. I figured it was time to leave when he asked me if I'd like to snort some coke in the men's room.

Chapter Four

I was more than a little turned off by Pope, and this soured my interest in the deal. On the other hand, I wasn't very tired when I got back to the hotel and was in a reading mood, so I started to look over the prospectus. There were two sections—a synopsis of the movie with illustrations up front and a financial breakdown at the back. I looked over the numbers at the back. Whoever had put them together knew their business. It was a solid deal. If I separated out my bad feelings toward Pope, it was precisely the kind of deal I had been looking for.

I read the synopsis of the film itself and liked it.

Called *Crash,* it opened on the coast of Ireland in the present time. A young American reporter and his girlfriend were taking a skin-diving holiday. The reporter's hobby was researching sunken ships. In this case, they were looking for a small Spanish cargo ship that had run into a mine left over from World War I and had sunk in 1938 just off the Irish mainland.

The reporter and his girlfriend find the ship and discover something that strikes them as peculiar. The hull of the ship has been blown in at a number of points, not just at one, as one would expect with a mine.

Back on land, the reporter digs deeper. As he does, he begins to uncover an incredible plot and counterplot hatched more than forty years before and conveniently buried by the confusion of the Second World War.

The main story of the film itself is the plot and

counterplot, set in 1938. In that year, the Nazis conspire with a group of Irish Republican Army officials to supply them with the necessary arms to mount an effective take-over of Northern Ireland.

The payment for the arms and subsequent support for the IRA activities is to be the assassination of King George VI by the IRA. The IRA has no qualms about making such a deal. They get a commitment from the Germans that on completion of the contract, the Germans, through their allies in Spain, are to arrange for the arms shipment to be sent from that country by boat. In mid-crossing, the IRA faction is to board the ship and sail it the rest of the way to Ireland.

Unknown to the Irish, the Germans are, at that time, secretly wooing the British. The Nazis have, in fact, concocted the scheme to show, first, the effectiveness of the Nazi espionage machinery, and second, their eagerness to have the British on their side.

The British Secret Service goes along with the plot in order to effectively trap and destroy a particularly radical wing of the IRA. The assassination attempt on King George VI is aborted on the day of the attack by the British Secret Service, and a news blackout is put up around the Royal Family for twenty-four hours.

The IRA believes the plot has been carried out and leaves secretly from the Irish coast to make the appointed rendezvous with the weapons-carrying ship sent by the Nazis from Spain.

Unknown to the IRA, Nazi frogmen have planted electromechanical devices wired to explosives to the hull of the ship and timed to go off before the ship reaches the Irish coast.

The IRA contingent reaches the ship, boards it, and heads for Northern Ireland as planned. British warships are put on the alert when it looks as though the explosives have not been set properly. One cutter gives chase to the Spanish ship and is badly shot up.

It looks as though the Spanish ship will, in fact, make it to Northern Ireland, but as the boat nears the coast, the explosives detonate, sending all on board, along with their shipload of guns, to the bottom of the sea.

The British send out the story of a Spanish ship lost at sea in a freak accident. They secretly thank the Nazis for their part in helping wipe out the IRA faction and, of course, never do get in bed with the Germans.

I had no trouble picking out the part Catherine St. Catherine would play. The lead female role was a Mata Hari figure, half-German, half-English, who makes contact with the British government on behalf of the Nazis and also sets up the deal with the IRA. The male lead is a British officer who, working undercover, has infiltrated the IRA and is caught up in going along with the Nazi connection to keep his cover. He is also carrying on a torrid love affair with the leading lady.

From what I could see, it looked like a solid adventure picture with a good mix of action, intrigue, sex, and chase.

I was intrigued with the project but still smarting from the session with Pope. I turned out the light and played the movie through in my head once or twice before I fell asleep.

Chapter Five

The nice thing about having money in your pocket is the embarrassment of choice. Before you spend it, invest it, piss it away or whatever, you have an infinite number of possibilities. The difference between the rich and poor is not just the material possessions but the options.

I was cash rich for the moment. Pope's deal looked good. On the other hand, there were other possibilities. Low-income housing and oil exploration offered some nice tax breaks. Not quite as good as the films but still worth considering.

I was having breakfast downstairs in the hotel dining room when I saw her come in. She spoke with Jimmy for a moment. He led her to my table. Even with her sunglasses on, you could see she was somebody. She turned every head in the dining room.

"May I please sit down?" a very subdued Catherine St. Catherine asked in a voice not very many decibels above a whisper.

I nodded and stood while Jimmy held the chair for her.

He offered her the menu. She waved it away.

"Just Perrier and orange juice," she said. Jimmy gave the order to Helen, who was looking after my section that morning.

"I don't think I could eat a thing after last night," she confided to me. She took off her sunglasses. "I guess it's one way of keeping my diet."

Catherine St. Catherine is one of those women who looks good even when they look bad. I had no idea what was going on inside the lady's body, but the outside didn't look any the worse for wear. Before I had a chance to tell her she looked okay, one of the hotel guests came up and asked if she was Catherine St. Catherine.

When she said yes, he asked her if she'd mind signing some autographs. Not one but four. Three kids and the wife.

Catherine fumbled in her purse for a pen and some paper. I got to see the nice side of the lady. There was no hostility or condescension in her manner. She patiently asked him for the names of each of the kids and the wife, and threw in an extra one for the old boy himself. He gushed thanks to the point of embarrassment. Luckily he had the social good sense not to invite himself to sit down.

When he'd gone back to his own table, I asked, "Does that sort of thing bother you?"

"It used to when I was on my way up. I hung around with a lot of people who thought it was chic to think that everybody who watches television, goes to the movies, or believes in Hollywood has the I.Q. of an Edith Bunker. After I made it, I wised up. I realized we were all in it together, all living part of the great big fantasy that the other one dreams about. You know I hope that guy really is happily married and really loves those kids. That's what I dream about. And why not? Wishing good things doesn't cost any more, does it?"

She smiled and gave a little shrug before she continued. "You must think I'm pretty awful after last night."

"I think you're a bad drunk," I said, "and I haven't seen enough of you sober yet to have an opinion on that, but what I've seen so far, I like."

"About last night . . ."

"No need explaining yourself," I interrupted.

"I want to explain," she insisted.

"Okay, explain if you feel you have to."

"This picture is important to both Lazlo and myself. Both of our careers could use a real success to get back on track. If it fails, who knows when we'll get another chance. We're both very nervous. We were just letting off steam. Do you understand?"

I nodded.

"There's more," she went on before I could say anything to reassure her. "Do you know about Pope and me?"

"Only what I've read in the papers. I'm not a big movie fan."

"The shoot-up?"

I nodded again.

She smiled understandingly. "There's nothing like success to bring two people who really care for each other back together again. We're trying. It's difficult, but we've been trying for more than a year. I really love him, you know."

I didn't. And I really didn't care one way or the other. I don't get turned on by other people's affairs. I was beginning to wonder why she was even bothering to tell me all this.

"I'm telling you all this," she said, as if reading my mind, "because Lazlo was too embarrassed by what happened last night to face you. He knows you're pretty influential in certain financial circles. He doesn't want you as an enemy."

"So, he sent you to make peace."

"I insisted I come. I wasn't exactly the queen of the ball last night either," she said, then added, "Lazlo would like to see you to say he's sorry."

"Tell him to drop by, anytime."

"He's outside, waiting in a taxi. He wants to apologize. He just doesn't know how. He's so damned European about these things sometimes."

"You tell him if he wants to apologize, that's okay. If he doesn't, that's okay, too. I really don't care one way or the other."

"Then you'll go with him?" she asked in a very cheery little-girl voice.

"Go where?" I looked at her curiously.

"I'm sorry." She flushed. "My brain's only half dried out from last night. I forgot to tell you. Lazlo has made an appointment for you to meet Michael Jon Bridges this morning. That is, if you-still want to."

"Michael Jon Bridges?"

"Lazlo's producer. You *are* still interested in the project, aren't you?"

"I'm curious."

"In that case, let's not waste any more time."

She was up and out of her seat in a second. She swept me along with her to the door, chattering happily about how good the project was and tugging gently on my sleeve.

Chapter Six

The taxi with Pope inside was parked in front of the hotel. Pope opened the back door and leaned his head out. He had not fared as well as Catherine from the night before. His complexion was gray and his eyes were bloodshot. Dark bags hung under them like dirty laundry.

"Come on, Billy, get in. I got it all set up," he told me enthusiastically.

Catherine walked to the door of the cab, leaned in, and kissed Pope on the forehead.

"Gotta run, darling," she said to him, then turned to me, wiggled her fingers, and smiled a cutesy good-bye.

"See you later," she said, blowing me a kiss. She waved down a cab going by on the other side of the street, then darted across the street, jumped in the back of the cab, and was gone a moment later.

Pope was still holding the door open for me, looking like a puppy dog that needed a friend.

I climbed in beside him. He smiled and slapped me on the back.

"Ain't it a great day?" He laughed heartily, breathing a foul stink of alcohol masked faintly by mint-flavored toothpaste.

"Tell me about Michael Jon Bridges," I said.

"You're going to like him, Billy. He's your type." Pope gave the driver the address on Yonge Street and then began to fill me in.

For someone as self-centered as Pope, it was almost

refreshing to hear him talk about Michael Jon Bridges with the kind of reverence he usually reserved for himself.

Bridges, according to Pope, was a colossus. He *was* London Bridges Productions of England before it sold out to the Sheppard Studios. Bridges was known as the British equivalent of Joseph E. Levine. Bridges had produced over three hundred pictures in the past forty years. Pope ran through two dozen from memory, and I recognized more than half. A few I had seen at the Saturday matinee when a double feature cost thirty-five cents. A few, like his remake of Jack London's *White Fang* and his adaptation of Mark Twain's *Mysterious Stranger,* were considered classics of their genre and were studied in cinema schools on both sides of the Atlantic. *The Wayward Journey* was probably his greatest critical success. It had earned Maria Tessier the best actress award at the Cannes Film Festival a few years back.

Bridges had been in show business all his life. His real name was Hyman Bernhardt; he was a distant cousin of the great Sarah Bernhardt. Orphaned at ten, he paid for his keep touring the vaudeville circuits as a child actor specializing in impersonations of famous people.

He eventually changed his name to Michael Jon Bridges to sound more English, less Jewish, and turned from acting to producing when the cuteness of his youth had worn off and turned his career into a second-rate warm-up act.

He produced his first movie with Austrian financing just before the beginning of the Second World War and pocketed all the profits when war was declared. He'd used that first money to bankroll his next picture, and never looked back. According to Pope, he'd sold out his interests in Europe a year before and had come to Canada in search of a new venture. Pope had heard he was in town and had taken his project to Bridges. The rest, as they say, was history.

We arrived at Bridges's offices at eleven. He had a suite on the top floor of the Parker Building, one of the few downtown buildings which still had uniformed elevator operators.

Bridges's office looked like he'd just moved in. There were boxes piled everywhere. A secretary sat in the front room typing. She nodded to Pope as we walked by. She didn't bother to announce us. Pope opened the door to the inner office and ushered me in ahead of him.

The inner office was also in a state of chaos. The floor was littered with stacks of *Variety, Hollywood Reporter, Wall Street Journal, Financial Times, Barron's. Business Week, Economist, Far Eastern Economic Review,* and other center-line business journals and film trade papers. Film cans and reels of film were piled up high like Greek columns between the stacks of magazines and boxes. Several early nineteenth-century English hunt scenes lay unpacked, leaning against their wooden packing crates, waiting for someone to hang them up.

About the only thing that looked functional in the room was the big desk and the telephone. Bridges was on the phone when we came in. He was holding the receiver to his ear and listening while he drummed a pencil on the desk top.

After the build-up Pope had given me, Bridges looked much different from the colossus I had been expecting. He looked twenty years older than his fifty-eight years. His clothes were so old they were almost back in fashion. There was a dark stain in the middle of his tie and a matching one on his right jacket sleeve. His skin had the look of new bubble gum, all pink with a dusting of white powder on top. When he smiled, there were a number of long gaps between teeth on the sides.

The only redeeming thing about that face was the eyes. They more than made up for the rest. They were bright, alive, and had the mischievousness of a three-year-old and the wisdom of a sage all wrapped together.

He got off the phone and stood up. He wasn't much over five feet in his stocking feet. That's exactly what he was in when he walked around the desk to greet me. He shook my hand vigorously.

"Excuse the mess. It'll get worse once we start shooting." He chuckled as he cleared a space on a side table by dumping several stacks of file folders on the floor. He moved two chairs alongside each other at the table.

I had to like Bridges. He didn't waste time. Three minutes after I'd arrived in the office, Pope had left, and Bridges and I were seated at the side table looking at the numbers. We worked backward from the bottom line through the costs, contingencies, and investment structure. Then he walked me all the way forward to the projections for profits and losses based on North American and world theatrical distribution, television, cable, cassettes, and commercial spin-offs like the sound track and other areas.

According to Bridges the five-million-dollar completion cost of the film would be picked up by presales to foreign distributors and television, meaning North America would be all gravy and money in our pockets. The film wouldn't be released for at least a year after principal photography was completed. Profits would be deferred another year, meaning there would be a tax write-off for the investors for two years and profits in years three, four, five, and on if the film was a smash.

"All we have to do is make it, to make money." Bridges smiled.

He made it all sound so easy. The five million dollars would be spent on the script, talent and crew costs, equipment rentals, sets, film stock and laboratory costs, editing time, and all the other costs that would turn out two cans filled with about ten thousand feet of celluloid worth a few thousand dollars without the pictures on it.

Two million of the five was coming from the local subsidiary, a U.S. distributor called National Pictures. National was the recent creation of two merged film companies, which made it the fourth largest film company in the world, in the same league as Universal, Paramount, Warner, Twentieth-Century, and Columbia. Like most of the big ones, it was owned by a larger diversified multinational. In National's case, its parent was Unico Industries of New Jersey, a big-board listed conglomerate with interests in food processing, computers, aerospace technology, prefabricated housing, and enter-

31

tainment. It made the Fortune 500 in 1970 and was currently at 123 and gaining. It was as solid as diamonds.

The second two million of the five was coming from the federal government's film fund, run by the newly reorganized Department of Economic Development.

Of the one million dollars remaining, eight hundred and fifty thousand had been raised through a public offering in lots of twenty-five thousand each.

"Mostly dentists from Winnipeg with one piece each," Bridges explained.

Even though they were still a hundred and fifty thousand dollars shy of the projected costs, they had passed the go point at four and a half million.

"We actually expect to raise more than the five in the long run," Bridges explained. It would give the investors an immediate payback or a chance to roll the money into a second project Bridges had on the boards.

"Filmmaking's the biggest crap shoot in the world." Bridges laughed. "When you're hot, you keep rolling and rolling. The trick between smart and dumb is knowing when that bad roll means the streak is over or you're just in the middle of a little breathing space. The secret of gambling is being a smart quitter."

I liked what I was seeing. The numbers looked great. I'd already made up my mind on the story itself. I liked it. The more I thought about it, the more I could see it as good solid entertainment. Bridges backgrounded me on the writer. His name was Harold D. Kessler. He was a well-known *Toronto News* investigative reporter. He and Pope had been working on the script for over a year.

"Can I read the full script?" I asked.

"What are you, some kind of literary critic?" Bridges looked askance.

"Just curious," I assured him.

Reading the script in its entirety was impossible, he explained. Pope never let anyone see the full script. Even the actors and actresses who signed only saw the synopsis and a few odd pages from the full script. Not letting anyone see the full script was a convention that Pope had picked up in the States. It was used by a number of

New York and Hollywood directors, including Academy Award winner Woody Allen.

"But you must have seen the script to be able to sell it," I insisted.

Bridges laughed and picked up the phone book on the end of his desk. "With the right packaging I could sell the yellow pages as a remake of *Gone with the Wind.*

Chapter Seven

I left Bridges's office two hours and forty-five minutes later and a lot smarter. The shoddiness of his physical appearance had completely receded behind the dynamics of the man himself. I'd already given him a strong "maybe" from my side for three reasons—the numbers looked good, I needed the tax write-off, and I liked the man.

I left Bridges's building and was walking toward the taxi stand on the corner when I ran into Dani Davis. She was wearing a fur jacket, jeans, and no make-up and was carrying two armloads of packages. Even without trying, she was turning heads, both male and female. She had that special kind of alive quality that people can't help noticing and admiring. Certainly I couldn't. She didn't notice me until I said hello. Then she looked up at me and smiled, not quite able to place me at first.

"Hi, remember me?" I said.

"Sure, you're what's-his-name from last night," she said, then laughed at her own little joke.

I frowned disappointedly.

"Just kidding," she assured me, pointing a free finger like a gun. "Billy Nevers, right?"

I nodded.

"Sorry we had to cut it short, but I guess you can understand."

"Sure, what are friends for anyway." I could see she was beginning to juggle her packages to keep them from slipping. "Here, let me give you a hand," I said, offering to help.

"No, I'm all right, really," she assured me as she set the bags down and stuffed several of the smaller ones into the largest bag. "I'm quite independent."

I asked her if she had time to finish our drink from the night before. I suggested we could Dutch it if she thought that would help her independence.

"I'd really like to, Billy, but I'm meeting some people and I'm already late."

"Maybe some other time," I said as she started walking away.

She just smiled back as she disappeared through the sidewalk crowd.

"Meeting somebody else," when they seemed to like you and didn't invite you along, usually meant "another guy." I wouldn't be surprised if she was hooked up with someone. These days you don't find that many good-looking women running around on the loose. In any case, I wasn't going to lose sleep over it. Maybe I'd see her again. She had the nicest smile, showing a big space between her two front teeth. Someone once told me that meant luck. I couldn't remember who told me, or whether the luck was supposed to be good or bad. I was in one of those moods when I figured it had to be good. Everything else was accelerating on the up-curve.

I wasn't so up, though, that I was a blind believer. There was one thing about the deal that bothered me. The lack of signed contracts. There were a number of letters of intent but no definitive contracts. Bridges had laughed that off. "In this business the only thing that's worth anything is your word. The lawyers will still be drawing up the contracts long after we've drawn down the money and shot the picture."

I made some calls to friends and people who owed me favors in Los Angeles and London. To the last one, they confirmed everything Pope had said about Bridges. He was an industry legend with a track record.

Herm Pynkis, a lawyer friend of mine in Los Angeles, allayed my fears about the lack of signed contracts. Pynkis was a senior partner in Amsley and Rogers, a prestigious West Coast law firm that handled a lot of film business. Pynkis summed it up for me: "You're talking about fast money, Nevers. You raise five or ten mill in three months and spend it in two. Like they say in the Westerns, fast money shoots from the hip. It doesn't have time to take aim.

"Besides, taking aim doesn't necessarily mean anything anyway. Look at *Cleopatra*. Twenty million in clever planning that turned to garbage. A million on a little picture like *Rocky* and it makes a hundred on the gross. In this business, a track record means your word's been tested and you're good."

"What do you know about Bridges?"

"Michael Jon Bridges?"

"The very same."

"He's had his ups and downs, but he's solid professionally."

"Ups and downs?"

"He's had some hits and some bombs, but I'd say more of the former than the latter. He makes money. If you're looking for real, he's real. If he couldn't make a five million deal over the telephone, he never would have survived the business for forty years."

"So you think he's good," I said.

"He's good, but that doesn't mean I'd put my money up. Every movie's a risk. The only thing I can tell you is to go by your own instincts."

"My instincts say he's solid," I said.

"On a business level, I'd say you're probably right," Pynkis assured me, "but I wouldn't advise you to hang out with him socially."

"How come?"

"They say he's a kink. You know, whips, chains, young girls under sixteen, amyl nitrate, coke. Lots of that sort of thing."

I thanked Pynkis for the advice. I didn't have any reason to believe or disbelieve the rumors about Bridges's personal life. I really couldn't care less. I wasn't interested in holding his hand. I was interested in the deal and that looked solid.

Chapter Eight

It was a busy week for me. Besides the calls, I was out at the hydroponics plant every day. The project was in the hands of a young and very competent industrial designer named Jane Willson.

The plant looked like the building of the Pharaoh's pyramids. The lethargy that usually hovers over any kind of building project just wasn't there. Everybody was working and working hard. What's more, they all seemed to be enjoying it from the hellos I got and the smiles on the faces around the building. The credit had to go to Ms. Willson, who was every bit as good a people manager as she was an engineer.

I sat in for her in the office and worked the budgets to give her more time to supervise the construction. It was at a critical stage. They were in the middle of pouring the concrete and laying the pipes for the irrigation system. Jane had developed a new system to conserve water through a new type of filtration duct. She wanted to spend all her time making sure it was perfect.

Knowing how conscientious she was, I figured if she spent that much time in the concrete, she'd probably spend all night in the office. And never complain. I came in to relieve her from the office work to relieve my own conscience. I figured I'd do my little bit so she could go home nights and be with the hubby and her five-year-old daughter.

I thought a lot about Bridges, Pope, and the film

deal, but it somehow kept getting pushed out of the way. I never got around to picking up the phone.

Pope finally called me ten days after I'd had the meeting with Bridges. He wanted to know how I was, what I thought of the film deal, and whether or not I was free for dinner that evening.

I told him I was fine, I hadn't made up my mind on the deal, and I wasn't sure about dinner.

"You're still mad about the last time, aren't you?"

I didn't answer. He caught me flat-footed on that one. I wasn't especially interested in babysitting a couple of drunks again.

"Listen, Billy, we're off the hard and heavy. I swear. We're too close to shooting time to risk a binge."

I felt kind of low for still holding a grudge, so I agreed to go to his place for dinner. There was no good reason not to give him the benefit of the doubt.

I arrived at Pope's place at six with a bottle of twenty-five-year-old Napoleon brandy as a peace offering. Pope's apartment was different than I imagined it. I had expected chrome and glass. Instead I was treated to a fine old collection of eighteenth-century armoires, a hand-rubbed monk's table, and assorted other pieces that looked museum quality.

Catherine St. Catherine was fluttering between the kitchen and the sitting rooms playing the perfect hostess. She looked as grand as ever. She gave me a big hug and kiss and took my coat.

Pope, dressed in a checkered apron, was fiddling with the barbecue he'd set up in the fireplace. He spent his time flitting like some giant insect between the grill and the adjacent sitting room, using his grill fork for a pointer whenever he wanted to emphasize something.

Bridges was in the adjacent room talking to Farrell King. I'd never met King, but I knew who he was. In the last six months, he'd made the covers of *Time* and *Newsweek* twice. You could hardly turn on the TV without seeing him as a guest on one of the talk shows or blockbuster specials. King had been in more than twenty films in the past six years, but he'd finally caught the public eye in a remake of *Teacher's Pet*. He won an

Academy Award for best actor and became an overnight household word.

Bridges introduced me and asked me to join them. Bridges and Pope were both trying to convince King to take the male lead in *Crash*. It was quite entertaining to watch Pope and Bridges work over King like the good and bad cops. Bridges, the bad cop, talked about money, percentages, and patriotism. King had been born and raised in Moosejaw, Saskatchewan, and was still a Canadian citizen. The citizenship was important in order to guarantee enough Canadian content in the film to allow the generous tax deductions.

Pope talked about King's career.

"Think what it would mean if you won an Oscar two years in a row," Pope taunted him. "Why, the part is so good a deaf mute could give a four-star performance. Think what an actor of your talents could do with it."

King put on a good show for Pope, asking him about the script and particularly about the character King was being asked to play. But it was easy to see his first interest lay with Bridges and the money. There was something about the eyes, a kind of dull listlessness, that gave him away. Bridges was ruthlessly persistent, playing on King's greed and obvious insecurity over money.

"Do you know how many one-hit movie men there are out there who haven't worked since the first and only big one?"

When King didn't answer, Bridges continued.

"Thousands, my good man, thousands. When they finally got around to choosing the perfect part in the perfect movie, nobody wanted them anymore. The public had forgotten them, and the people in the business had more than their fill of their complaints and bitchiness. Your stock in trade is to keep working. Show them what you can really do, and be smart enough about your money to be able to save enough to retire on it when *you* decide you've had enough."

King was the hottest thing since John Travolta, but he knew what Bridges was saying. The public was fickle. If you didn't give them what they wanted or if their tastes changed and you didn't change with them, they'd drop you overnight. King needed a second hit. He wanted to know how Bridges was going to guarantee that. Bridges walked him through the promotion budget. From the questions King was asking, it was obvious that he only understood half of what Bridges was saying. But it didn't really matter. King would send in a small army of agents and lawyers if he liked the deal. This was just a dry run.

We were just sitting down to dinner when Dani showed up. A nice surprise.

King was introduced, and he mustered all the charm of an old-time matinee idol. He kissed her hand and told her, "I've heard so much about you. All of it good."

It made her laugh nervously. She glanced at me and gave me a warm, "How are you, Billy?"

From the way King took her hand and led her to the dinner table, it was obvious he had designs on her. He put on a remarkable show. He name-dropped and told intimate little stories about life in Moosejaw and Hollywood. He had anecdotes about everyone from Frank Sinatra to Richard Dreyfuss. He charmed us right through the lobster appetizer, chateaubriand, and chocolate mousse dessert.

I was a pedestrian in the world they were talking about. Bridges exchanged stories about the young Laurence Olivier. Pope talked about the time he'd made a movie with Raquel Welch. Catherine had her stories about Warren Beatty and Burt Reynolds, and even Dani had a funny story to tell about George Segal! When one would finish, someone else would jump in and begin telling a more outrageous story. I felt like I was speed-reading two years' worth of *Confidential* magazine. The stories went on long after the meal and continued after we had retired to the living room. Catherine opened the bottle of brandy, and King dug half a dozen joints out of his jacket pocket. Pope and Catherine had one glass of brandy each and a couple of puffs of the first joint that circled the room. They both seemed to be looking self-consciously to me for approval of their self-control. It embarrassed me, but on the other hand, I was glad there wouldn't be a repeat of the scene in the Lazy Susan. Bridges drank his brandy from a large glass and declined the pot. Dani was heavy on the brandy and light on the grass, the same as me. I took a couple of puffs of the weed as it made the rounds. A little bit of good grass could give me a nice edge at times. I was careful not to smoke too much, though. The few times that I had, I'd ended up feeling like muscular dystrophy looks. King drank and smoked everything. He swilled the brandy and chain-smoked four of the six joints by himself. Nothing seemed to have any effect on him. He just kept smiling and talking a mile a minute, which is what he'd been doing most of the evening anyway.

After the brandy was gone, Bridges fell asleep in a chair by the fireplace and started to snore so loudly it gave us all the giggles. We laughed so loud that we finally woke him up. He yawned, said his good nights, and left.

I was thinking about leaving myself. Catherine and Pope were mostly talking about the film. King had cornered Dani on the couch and was laying on the charm. Before I got a chance to make my move, King announced he was going.

It didn't surprise me that King should ask Dani to leave with him. From the build-up he'd been giving her all evening, it was a foregone conclusion that he expected her to leave with him.

What surprised me was that she turned him down. Politely, but flatly, with no question of being talked into it. King smiled like a sore loser and left.

I figured she'd stay a while, then escort Catherine home. Catherine and Dani made small talk for a little while until Pope started yawning. I'd let enough time lapse since King had left to make my own exit without running into him on the sidewalk.

I stood up to leave and was in the middle of thanking everybody for a pleasant evening, when Dani stood up too.

"Would you mind giving me a ride home?" she asked.

41

"Love to," I said and turned to Catherine, half expecting her to go along too. She answered my question without my having to ask it.

"I'm staying." She smiled and took Pope's arm and pulled him out of his seat. We said our good-byes standing up, and two minutes later Dani and I were walking along the sidewalk toward my car.

She slipped her arm through mine and said, "I'm not very tired, and if you don't mind, I'd be interested in having that drink you promised me."

She said it in a way that told me she'd made up her mind long before the evening began that I was going to take her home.

There were a few after-hours' places open, but she insisted we'd be more comfortable at my place. "I'm interested in how you live," she told me.

So, we drove straight there. We drank and talked and talked, about anything and everything. I felt really comfortable with her, like I'd already known her a long time. Mostly it was her sense of humor. She laughed in the right spots. She was like a fresh breeze in my life. I was too old to fall in love that quickly, but I'd never be too old to fall into a healthy like. And I did like this one.

When it came time to go to bed, there wasn't a lot of bullshit about whether we should or shouldn't or could or couldn't. We both wanted to. Not because it was easy and available, but because it would be a nice thing to do with each other.

There's a funny myth about men, that they like the challenge. The only time anyone needs that kind of challenge is when they're chasing something they don't really want. Any man who knew what he was after never took any points in scoring off someone who didn't want him.

The greatest part of being with someone is mutual attraction. For two people who know who they are and where they're coming from, it's natural to let what's happening really happen. Without a lot of conditions and expectations like all that "What do I get for this; what do you get for that?" nonsense that usually accompanies intercourse.

I don't mean coming together is physically easy or something you take for granted. There was a certain awkwardness and shyness for both of us. But that didn't last long, and it didn't keep us from enjoying each other. She was one of those rare women whom I'd run into in my life that I wanted to make love to *and* sleep with. Sometimes you can't separate out the two, but you know you don't quite feel right doing one or the other. Maybe that's because sex is so alive and awake, and sleep is the sad little brother of death. You don't necessarily always want to do all things with all people. With this one I could do it all and feel good the whole time.

Chapter Nine

Dani and I spent a lot of time together in the next few days. Jane Willson had put her foot down and told me nicely that I was starting to cramp her style, so I phased myself out of the day-to-day operations at the hydroponics plant. Bridges still had his office downtown, but a second production office had been set up out at the Kleinberg Studios north of town. Dani was involved designing the sets, so I drove her out twice and hung around to get a feel of what was going on. The art department was busy creating the sets. Bridges was still interviewing a bevy of young actors and actresses. Costume designers were running in and out with designs. Pope was sequestered with Harold D. Kessler, working on story boards and revisions to the script. I met Kessler briefly on one occasion. He was a dark, moody little fellow who didn't have much to say to anyone and who never smiled or looked you directly in the eye. I didn't care for him, but Pope had complete confidence in his writing talents.

I spent most of the evenings with Dani, and three times we were a six-some with Catherine and Pope and Bridges and his date. Bridges's date was always a different one of the actresses who had come to the daytime casting sessions. They were always somehow alike. Cheap, tarty makeup, fashionably dressed in pants that were baggy on top and so tight at the ankles the girl probably had to unscrew her feet at night to get them off. It was obvious that Bridges wasn't interested in good conversation with the girls because not one of them was capable of stringing more than four words together in a row. Bridges was, nevertheless, good conversation on his own. He was constantly dazzling us with stories about his vaudeville days, about shooting films in the Soviet Union after World War Two, or some other equally entertaining bit. Once, in an offhanded manner, I asked how they were coming with their negotiations with Farrell King. I was wondering how Dani's rejection of King had affected the negotiations. Bridges assured me that King was only interested in the money. If they could come up with a deal that satisfied his agents, then King would do it. Dani spent several evenings at her place alone or with Catherine. She tried once or twice to explain that she needed some time by herself, but I told her the one thing she didn't have to do was a lot of explaining to me. No matter how close two people become, there are always some edges that you can't really share, at least not at the beginning. If you try to force things that aren't quite ready to fall into place, it can cause bad times and hard feelings down the road.

We were together enough for the enthusiasm of the film to wear off on me. At the beginning of the second week, I went to see Bridges with my cashier's check for two hundred thousand dollars. Bridges drew up the papers and signed over the eight shares of the film to me by the following day. I was effectively in the movie business. I was beginning to think it was one of the smartest moves I had ever made.

Had I waited another twenty-four hours, I would have changed my mind completely and never gotten involved in the picture.

Chapter Ten

I was sitting in my hotel room late the following afternoon, going over some paper work. I was waiting for Dani to show up for dinner. She'd called from the studio and said she'd be stopping off at her place first to pick up a few things and then would come by about five.

By six she hadn't shown up. I'd finished all of my reading and decided to watch the news while I was waiting. I tuned in in the middle of the story, and it took me several minutes to put all the pieces together. An on-the-spot camera team was stationed in front of an apartment complex filming some sort of siege. Police in riot gear had cordoned off the street and were evacuating nearby buildings. A group of religious fanatics had taken up refuge in one of the penthouse apartments of the building and were hurling furniture and clothing out the window onto the street. The building looked familiar, but then any one of a thousand modern apartment complexes built in the last two years in a hundred cities in North America or even Europe looked just the same. There hadn't been enough shots of the police to identify them either. The location had probably been mentioned, but before I had tuned in.

It was only after the station switched back to the studio commentary that I realized why the whole scene looked familiar. It was a local apartment building, and those were city police. It was the apartment building where Dani and Catherine St. Catherine lived.

46

The story was still breaking, so the station was trying to organize the bits and pieces as they came in.

A religious cult known as the Flock of God had entered the apartment complex with rifles and dynamite around five o'clock. They had stormed the apartment of Catherine St. Catherine and had set various pieces of furniture on fire before hurling them from the eighteenth-story windows to the street below.

There was no word yet on the whereabouts of Catherine St. Catherine or Dani.

My first move was to call Dani's apartment. I got a recording telling me the number was temporarily out of service. Next I tried Pope, but his line was busy. I called the studio but was told that Bridges, Pope, Catherine, and Dani had all left early in the afternoon. Bridges hadn't gone back to his downtown office and wasn't at his hotel either. I tried Pope again, but the line was still busy. Meanwhile, the evening news had uncovered a background film on the Flock of God cult and was screening it.

The Flock had been established by a Reverend Davidson Smith, a self-anointed evangelical preacher who preached a literal interpretation of the Bible. The members of the cult lived in tight-knit clans spread out through Ontario. Manitoba, Upper New York State, and Michigan. They numbered about four thousand. They were violently opposed to television, radio, modern appliances, automobiles, communism, public schooling, and a vast array of other daily facts of life. Their only concession to modern technology was their fanatical obsession with guns and explosives, both of which they felt were necessary to protect their flock from assaults from without. There had been a number of occasions in the past twenty years when cult members had been arrested and vast stockpiles of rifles, dynamite, and ammunition seized. Despite the weapons obsession, the group rarely involved itself in violent acts of any kind. When it did, it was usually an internal matter among church members. All those who joined the Flock, or were born to parents who were members, were considered to be members for life—whether they wanted to be or not. If the other members felt that a member was straying too far from the flock, it was their duty to do everything in their power to bring that member back into the fold.

The newscast showed some old footage of a split-level home in the city's suburbs which had been razed to the ground several years before by members of the Flock of God. The house had been occupied by a Flock member who had given up the church and had gone into the dry cleaning business in the city. For six years he had quietly endured threats on his and his family's life but had grown to accept it. The final straw came when the man began advertising his service on television. The Flock members found out about it and set the house and his business on fire.

Reverend Smith and several members of the church were convicted and sent to jail. During the next six years, the Flock of God Church witnessed a drastic decline in its membership, with many members fleeing the area and leaving no forwarding addresses.

The Reverend Smith had been released from jail eighteen months ago and had begun to quietly rebuild his church. This was the first time since he had been freed from jail that he had caught the public's attention.

I tried one last time to get through to Pope. When I couldn't, I hopped in the car and headed for Dani's apartment. On the way over, I flipped the buttons on the radio, trying to get the latest coverage. Bits and pieces of the story were still coming in. There were unconfirmed reports that either Catherine or Dani were members of the cult. There were other rumors that it was a case of mistaken identity. One station had it that the Reverend Smith was inside the apartment and another station said that he'd been shot and killed. Still another station had it on good authority that nude pictures of Catherine St. Catherine, which had been published in *Love* magazine, Canada's answer to *Penthouse,* and which had hit the newsstands that afternoon, had provoked the attack.

I got within two blocks of the apartment complex before I got stopped. The police had cordoned off the area and were keeping everyone out. I used the name of my old friend Lieutenant Hagen to worm my way up to the front line. Hagen wasn't involved in the operation, but a buddy of his named Brogan was running the show from a corner candy store in the building opposite Catherine's and Dani's. He wasn't especially pleased to see me, but for the sake of Hagen's friendship filled me in on what he knew.

No one had been hurt. So far. The apartment had been empty when the cult had seized it. They weren't quite sure what demands the Flock of God people were making. The Reverend Smith was in the apartment. The group apparently had enough dynamite to blow off the top six floors of the building. Lastly, they knew that the siege had something to do with a five-page nude photo spread of Catherine St. Catherine, but no one knew exactly what. He handed me a copy of the magazine from the candy store rack. It fell open to the center spread showing Catherine St. Catherine with her legs spread, rubbing her hand over her naked crotch.

I flipped backward through the picture spread. It was supposed to be a special section on the film *Crash,* a pre-production spread, but that was just the come-on. It was just an excuse to run a very seedy series of pictures of Catherine. I didn't have to dig too deep to figure how she had allowed herself to pose for the shots. The photo credits listed Lazlo Pope.

I gave the magazine back to Brogan. There was no sense in my hanging around since neither of the girls was in the building. I tried calling Pope, but his line was still busy. I got back in my car and drove toward his place.

Chapter Eleven

I was greeted at Pope's apartment by a phalanx of gun-toting, walkie-talkie carrying security guards who were holding at bay two dozen news people from the daily press, radio, and television. I had to wait ten minutes for clearance before I got inside the building.

Bridges met me at the door in his bare feet, a big grin on his face. He was smoking a cigar the length of his forearm.

"Billy Nevers, why it's a pleasure to see you," he said, affecting an Irish lilt to his speech. "Come in and welcome to our little three-ring circus."

I could see from the doorway he wasn't kidding. They'd already selectively let in half the news teams in town. The National News team was setting up their cameras in one corner. The rival First Edition crew was setting up their equipment at the opposite end of the room. Several newspaper reporters were hanging around the other two corners, comparing notes and waiting for something to happen. One of Bridges's dates from the previous week was walking about the room, serving drinks from a large silver tray. Pope was in the middle of the room talking on the telephone. He saw me and gave me a big smile and mouthed the words, "How are you?" as he listened over the receiver. There were at least a half a dozen more security guards standing or sitting about the apartment. Two had their hats off and drinks in their hands. The other four looked like they were still pretending they were on duty.

Dani and Catherine were nowhere in sight.

"Where are they? Where are the girls?" I barked at Bridges, backing him into a corner. Out of the corner of my eye, I could see one of the security guards approaching us. Bridges waved him down.

"Take it easy, Billy, take it easy," Bridges tried to calm me. He was high but not quite drunk.

"Where're Dani and Catherine?" I insisted.

"They're all right, they're both all right. I swear to you." Bridges eyed me nervously.

Pope hung up the phone and came right over.

"That was AP, they're running it on the wire," Pope informed us excitedly. "*People* magazine wants to put us on the cover. Do you realize what this is going to do for the film?"

I'd just come from a building full of dynamite and armed lunatics. My girl was out there somewhere, maybe in a lot of trouble, and I was standing with two fruitcakes who wanted to talk about publicity. I was ready to hit somebody. And Pope was closest to my size.

"I've already seen enough of your publicity and your pictures," I said, grabbing Pope by the collar. I was mad enough to hit him if he hadn't gone totally limp on me. He turned chalk white and looked like he was going to throw up.

"The pictures were Catherine's idea," he gagged. Two security guards came toward us, but Bridges again waved them away. I let go of Pope and took a deep breath to calm myself.

"Where's Dani and Catherine?" I repeated myself.

The phone rang across the room. Bridges's bimbo girlfriend picked it up.

"It's *Newsweek*. Do you want to speak to them?" she yelled.

Pope nodded, rubbing his neck and looking at me. Bridges nudged Pope toward the phone, then stepped between him and me.

"You can talk to Dani from the private line in the bedroom," Bridges said in a low whisper so no one else could hear. "She's with Catherine. They're under guard at the Airport Motor Inn. We thought it would

51

be best to keep them out of the limelight until things calm down a bit. They're registered under Martin Rogers."

I walked into the bedroom. I expected to be alone. Instead I walked in on a second one of Bridges's bimbos and a security guard, both half undressed with their hands in each other's pants. I threw them both out half dressed.

I used the second line to dial the motor inn. There was a Martin Rogers registered, but the party had left word they didn't wish to be disturbed. It took me twelve minutes to convince the security guard at the other end to tell Dani I was calling. I was just about ready to hang up, drive out to the motor inn, and storm the room when Dani finally came on.

"Hi, how are you? Sorry I'm late for dinner." She laughed. It was a nervous laugh, not all that happy.

"You okay?" I asked.

"I'll make it," she assured me. "It's damned good to hear your voice."

"You want me to come out there?"

"It's probably better if you don't. Catherine's pretty upset. I've got my hands full. Luckily I found I was able to talk one of the guards into parting with a couple of Valiums. I think she'll be okay."

"What about you?"

"I'm pretty independent, Billy. I don't get scared that easy," she assured me, just a little too tough.

"What's the connection to the Flock of God cult?" I asked her, trying to find out just how deep she was in.

"You better ask Pope," she said after a little pause. It sounded like something she might not be able to talk about in front of Catherine, so I didn't push it.

"As long as you're okay," I insisted.

"I'm okay. They've got a dozen security guards looking after us, and so far the press hasn't figured out where we are. What could be better?" She laughed, then added in a quiet little voice, "Billy, I miss you."

"I miss you, too," I told her. It was the first time I realized that I had been letting the relationship just happen. Now I had to think about it. I realized how attached I had grown to this one in such a short time.

We said our good-byes. There wasn't much either one of us could do until the situation resolved itself one way or the other. I could only guess how long that would take. There were still too many question marks.

Pope was just getting off the phone when I came out of the bedroom. Bridges was cracking a bottle of champagne. I was in no mood to party and went straight for Pope. Everyone in the room came to a full stop while they waited for me to make my move. I was still angry but not mad. Before I could say anything, Pope started explaining.

"We thought the pictures would be a good idea. You know, drum up a little pre-production publicity," Pope insisted and turned to Bridges for support.

Bridges came over with a champagne glass in hand. "We've gotten a million dollars' worth of publicity, Billy, and all of it free. We couldn't ask for more," he assured me.

I didn't care about the pictures. I wanted to know about the Flock of God. "What's the connection?" I insisted.

Pope and Bridges exchanged glances, then both tried to look at me but couldn't. They both glanced around at the media people who had gone back to the food and drink like they were covering a bar mitzvah.

"I suppose it's old news now," Bridges said to Pope. "It's been out on the wire service."

"What's the connection?" I insisted again.

It was Pope who finally told me. I realized afterwards that if I'd had a choice, I probably would have preferred not to know. What he told me sent an involuntary chill down my spine.

He looked at me and spoke the words with a nervousness in his voice that undercut the revelry: "The Reverend Davidson Smith is Catherine St. Catherine's father."

Chapter Twelve

Catherine St. Catherine's connection to Reverend Davidson Smith had been one of the best-kept secrets in Hollywood. Catherine's mother had divorced the Reverend Smith in 1955 and had remarried Julian St. Catherine of Peterborough, Ontario, the following year. Catherine had taken her stepfather's name. Her mother had died in 1967 and her stepfather a year later, the same year she had signed her first major film contract in the U.S.

She'd had no contact with her father or the Flock of God since her mother's divorce. At least that was the opinion of Pope. He never heard her mention the subject to anyone and only found out about it because she had emptied their joint bank account about three years before and donated the whole amount anonymously to the Reverend Smith Defense Fund. She had admitted to Pope at the time that it was simply an impulse on her part to relieve herself of some residual guilt she was harboring.

She had never brought the subject up again. Pope was completely clueless as to how the Flock of God people got hold of the magazine, and so quickly. *Love* magazine had just hit the stands that afternoon. It wasn't exactly the kind of reading material the Flock of God people were likely to come across on their own. Did the Reverend Smith have a subscription? Did the group have a special monitoring service? Or did someone conveniently send him the magazine? If so, who? It wasn't the kind of thing that Catherine would send home to dear old Dad. If I was to believe Pope, he didn't do it. According to him, he was just making the most of a bad situation. I had no real reason to believe him. On the other hand, it was the kind of thing that was nearly impossible to prove. I had no way of knowing who also knew about Catherine's past. I did have a hard time imagining anybody else being able to profit to the extent Pope was profitting. Except maybe Bridges. But then he swore he didn't know the connection between Catherine and Reverend Smith until the media got hold of it.

Luckily for all concerned, the bad situation didn't get worse. The police showed a commendable amount of restraint and simply decided to wait it out. After two days of the siege, the Flock of God people were willing to negotiate.

First, they demanded use of the public broadcasting system. The police agreed to let the network news teams enter the building.

Reverend Smith used the forum first to condemn the medium itself, calling television the scourge of modern society and the "eye of the devil." However, as a man of God, he felt that it was within his jurisdiction to use this eye of the devil to preach the truth. He spent the next hour condemning the evils of pornography. He mentioned by name *Love* magazine and the movie *Crash*. He promised that his people would do all in their power to continue to condemn that sort of thing and, where possible, would take action against the printing of such publications and the making of such movies.

"We dedicate ourselves to the war against the Antichrists and all those who condone unnatural acts against our Lord. We shall fight these evils whenever and wherever we can, with all our God-given strength," he told the television masses, shaking his fists high in the air. He was a remarkable sight to behold, even on the small screen. The Reverend Smith was six foot six, according to the news reports, and he towered over the newsmen and his followers by a full head. He was in his sixties but looked more like mid-forties. He had a full head of snow-white hair, which he wore shoulder length in the style of the biblical patriarchs. He had a well-kept beard and the fullest eyebrows I had ever seen. They were the size of a heavy mustache and he kept the ends turned up in great curly points.

He was at once commanding and frightening. I could easily imagine how, if this man's preachings were a little more to the left of crazy, he could persuade thousands by his electricity.

What struck me as strange about all his comments was that, although he repeatedly mentioned *Love* and *Crash* in his attack, he never once mentioned Catherine St. Catherine.

After the Reverend Smith had had his say over the networks, he and his six cohorts, who had laid siege to Catherine's and Dani's apartment, surrendered quietly to the police. The six included three young men and three young women, one of whom was about seven months pregnant.

In the final analysis, there had been no kidnaping, no major damage to property, and no violent crime. The guns were legally obtained. There was some question about the origin of the dynamite, but nothing could be proved.

At best, the district attorney was able to come up with a string of misdemeanors including trespassing, public mischief, and a few other minor charges.

In an effort to continue to milk the publicity, Bridges paid the bail for the Flock of God Seven. Reverend Smith told a gathering of reporters outside the detention center that he would turn all his efforts toward stopping the film.

"All those connected with this vile piece of filth will have to answer to God," he told his listeners. "God's reward for the sins of Sodom and Gomorrah was a fiery death. And so shall it be for those who practice the ways of the ancient disaffects."

Since no direct threats were made, the police were powerless to do anything about the veiled threats. Two days later, despite the conditions of their bond, the Flock of God had disappeared from sight. Newsmen were unable to find them and the police repeatedly issued "no comment" bulletins. I found out from my contacts at the station that they had put a five-man task force on the search but were not hopeful of finding anything. Their only reassurance was that they suspected the Flock of God would probably leave the city and quite possibly the country to avoid further confrontation with the judicial system that had jailed Reverend Smith. I wasn't so sure, but there wasn't much any of us could do.

Dani stayed with Catherine most of the time. They kept the Airport Motor Inn suite because it was close to the studio. Their apartment in town was a total loss, but the damage was mostly covered by insurance. I visited them on the set at the studio. They were still in pre-production. There wasn't that much going on, but Pope insisted that Catherine show up for her drama and dance lessons in order to keep her busy. There were half a dozen security guards stationed around the studio grounds. Two more were permanently assigned to Catherine.

Several media types also hung around the set. Bridges fed them and talked to them regularly, but they were under strict orders not to approach Catherine. She refused to talk about the incident publicly. Even the police could pry no more out of her than her insistence that she had no idea why Reverend Smith had singled her out at this time for his demonstration.

During the first two days after the siege ended, two of the media people tried to corner her to get more information. Both were ejected from the lot. By the third day, the story was old news and most of the media people had departed. By the fifth day, they had all gone.

I saw Dani a number of times, almost always with Catherine. It was apparent that Catherine was under a great deal of pressure. Her skin had turned blotchy, and she was making demands on everybody to bring her things and look after her personal needs. She fired and rehired her hairdresser four times in one day. Dani was keeping up a good front. She somehow managed to keep smiling as she apologized her way through the day to delivery people, Catherine's dermatologist, acting coach, dancing coach, wardrobe girl, and anyone else who got within range of Catherine's insults.

Catherine alternated between bouts of manic activity, when she thought everything was funny, and fits of depression, when she spoke of death and dying. Once Pope confided to me that he wasn't sure she'd be able to do the picture. Her psychiatrist was more reassuring. The shrink said Catherine was only reacting normally to a stressful situation but was basically as healthy as a horse. She just needed to talk out her feelings among friends.

I spent several evenings with Catherine, Dani, and Pope. Catherine did most of the talking. She shouted down or quietly ignored any comments anyone else made, so after a while we stopped making any. It was always the same story over and over.

"Isn't it more ungodly to be clothed?" she would ask, fidgeting nervously with the top button of her blouse. She would button and unbutton it a hundred times during an evening while she talked. "Does a father have the right to demand that his offspring live in his image as if he were God? Isn't that the most blasphemous act of all? To try to alter the human spirit on the assumption that you're more God-like than the rest of God's creatures."

Catherine's near incoherent ramblings were those of a very tortured soul. None of us could avoid being affected by her condition, but none of us could provide her with the answers either.

None of us had posed nude for the masses. If we were to take the Reverend Smith's vow at face value, everyone associated with the film was in danger. But Catherine had to be front and center among us. Hers was the sexy part in the film. The Reverend Smith was her father. None of us could comprehend the blood relationship between the two, despite the fact that they had not seen nor spoken to each other in more than two decades. She was her father's daughter. She had been born into the Flock and raised within it for the better part of her earliest formative years. Finally, there were the kinds of swings that she'd gone through from Hollywood star to has-been on the comeback trail in a five-year stretch. The drunken crudeness, the elegant sophistication, the generousness, brilliance, introspection, and bitchiness were all very real parts of the woman. Asking anyone to imagine what Catherine St. Catherine was going through was a little like asking what it feels like to be cottage cheese.

Chapter Thirteen

No one saw much of Bridges after the media left. He stayed in his downtown office most of the time. He continued to try to drum up interest in the story. At one time he even tried to sell the out-takes of the photo session with Catherine to *Playboy* magazine. It turned out the best of the photos had already gone to *Love*. What was left was garbage.

"You've got to use everything you've got," Bridges confided to me one time when we both happened to be at the Kleinberg studio. I'd been shuttling between the plant in Ajax and the studio for the better part of ten days, trying to lend some moral support to Dani.

Bridges also confided to me he was beginning to worry about Catherine's ability to do the film both because of the possibility of physical danger and her state of mind. But Catherine wasn't his only worry. Pope was also beginning to wear thin from the strain. He was edgy and had tried to goad Bridges into an argument on the few times he'd shown up on the set, claiming Bridges was mismanaging the production. He kept trying to get Bridges to commit to a firm date for principal photography to begin. Bridges kept waffling, insisting there was still some paper work to clear up.

I asked him about this, and he assured me there was no problem with the money. He was simply holding off production until he was sure that both Pope and Catherine would be able to go all the way. "I don't want the expense of changing directors or lead actresses in midstream," he insisted.

Pope spent a good deal of his time rationalizing the nude photo session of Catherine to all who would listen. He tried to convince Catherine that she had somehow contributed greatly to freedom of expression by becoming a public flasher. Behind her back, he called her crazy and spoiled and an outright bitch.

But Catherine was far from his only problem. During the days following the siege, a rift developed between Pope and Harold D. Kessler. The sullen screenwriter on several occasions got into loud arguments with Pope. It was always about the script. Kessler became increasingly vocal about the fact that Pope wanted to make a number of changes which Kessler thought would destroy the story. Watching these two was a little like watching a foreign film without the subtitles. They spoke in a kind of shorthand and never directly about the content of the script, at least not in public. They only spoke about what the other was doing to ruin the story. The arguments usually degenerated into petty name-calling, where one would accuse the other of immaturity, irrationality, naiveté, stupidity, pigheadedness, lack of taste or sensitivity or both, or any combination of insults that they could muster.

Toward the end of the first week after the siege, Pope began insisting the changes were necessary for financial reasons. I found this out because he tried to use me as cannon fodder in one of his arguments with Kessler.

"Do you think investors like Billy Nevers are into this picture to throw away money?" he asked Kessler in front of me.

"We got five million, that's more than enough to do it right," Kessler said, eyeing me with suspicion and hostility.

"It's enough to make a great picture if we don't waste it doing things that won't work cinematically."

"How the hell can you know what works and what doesn't until you try it?" Kessler insisted.

"That's the difference between being a professional and an amateur," Pope explained tiredly.

Kessler sneered.

"How the hell did I ever let myself get mixed up with a group of pikers like you," Kessler hissed at both of us.

"Because you need us," Pope said. "Now, be a good fellow and make the cuts."

"Damn it, man, those cuts are going to kill the whole story."

"Without those cuts, we'll never get it into the theaters," Pope scolded.

"Fuck the theaters."

"Fuck the theaters, and you fuck your meal ticket, asshole," Pope spat angrily. "Now, you go make those cuts or I'm going to make them for you. I can guarantee you won't like what I cut out."

Kessler went off in a black sulk, shooting me a hate-filled glance. When he'd gone out of earshot, Pope turned to me.

"He's overwritten the damned thing by fifty pages," he explained.

I'd already picked up enough to realize that fifty pages represented nearly an hour of extra film. At the current estimates of more than forty thousand dollars a minute, that worked out to more than a two-million-dollar overrun. I was sympathetic to Pope's arguments, but something in Pope's tone said it wasn't just an overrun problem.

"Are you having second thoughts about bringing the film in under the five million?" I asked him.

"Oh, Christ, no," he assured me. "I hope all that nonsense with Kessler hasn't gotten you worried."

I didn't answer. It's interesting how silence can sometimes shake the rats out of the basement faster than a lot of noise.

"Kessler's basically a good writer," Pope explained, "but he's like most writers. He needs to have his nuts kicked once in a while. He's not to be taken seriously. As far as the film is concerned, we're in great shape."

"No serious problems," I added in a tone that said I was beginning to have my doubts.

"None we can't handle," he assured me, clapping his arm around my shoulder. "Now, let's go see if Dani and Catherine are ready for dinner."

We were going to take them out later. As we walked toward the studio where Catherine was working out, Pope remarked in an offhand and casual manner: "Farrel King's turned us down for the picture. We'll have to find ourselves a new male lead."

His remark was just a little too offhand and casual to be accepted at face value.

Chapter Fourteen

Several times during the evening I tried to get Pope to tell me why Farrell King had turned down the part. Pope insisted that he liked the part but had other commitments.

"You mean the money wasn't enough," I said.

"We offered him his rate and a piece of the action," Pope assured me. "Farrell King's a name, not an actor. He wants to stay in goodie-goodie movies. That's where he's had his greatest success. That's where he figures he'll continue to make his impact."

Pope said he had some ideas on who could replace Farrell King; but he didn't want to talk about them just yet.

"We got enough Canadian content to go American or British if we wanted to," he told me. "We can get Kristofferson, O'Neil, DeNiro, anybody we want with a picture like this."

I wasn't as confident that it was going to be as easy as Pope said it was going to be. On the other hand, there was no sense keeping on his back. The four of us had a nice dinner together. Catherine and Pope left together to go back to his place for the first time since the siege. That left Dani and me alone together for the first time in a very long time.

"It's going to have to be your place." She laughed, snuggling up to me in the car. "They're still trying to put mine back together."

"You want to stop by your hotel and pick anything up?" I asked.

"No." She shook her head, yawned, and leaned up against me.

We hadn't talked much in nearly two weeks, but neither of us seemed to feel the need to. We rode back to my place in easy silence.

We hadn't been in my hotel more than five minutes when there was a knock on the door. Dani had just turned on some music and I'd just filled two snifters with brandy. She looked at me and I shrugged. I wasn't expecting anybody. The place was fairly soundproof, so unless someone knew I was in, they'd think I wasn't home.

The knock came again. Dani looked at the door and then at me.

"Ignore it, they'll go away," I said to her. It ran through my mind that the Flock of God people were out there somewhere. I thought of calling the hotel security, then thought better of it. I decided to ignore the knock.

Whatever was out there went away. Dani and I settled down on the couch, at opposite ends with just our bare feet touching. We'd been doing this for about a minute when the house phone rang. I wasn't going to answer it, but Dani kept insisting it might be important.

I picked it up. It was Moe at the desk. He said there was a man in the lobby who insisted on seeing me. He'd seen me come in, so he knew I was in the room.

"He says his name's Bridges, Michael Jon Bridges," Moe told me over the phone.

"Let me talk to him," I said.

"He says he won't talk to you over the phone. He insists on seeing you," Moe said.

"All right, send him up," I agreed reluctantly. I figured if Bridges had come all the way over to the hotel, something important was up. I told Dani.

"Do you want me to wait in the other room?" she asked.

"Sit where you are. Let's just play this by ear," I said, getting up to answer the knock at the door.

I opened the door, fully expecting to see Bridges. Instead I found myself facing Harold D. Kessler, the movie writer. He pushed past me into the room before I could say anything.

"Where's Bridges?" I asked.

"I called you," he informed me. "I figured you wouldn't let me in, but you'd see Bridges if it was an emergency. I was right."

"What's the problem?" I asked.

He smiled with half his mouth. His eyes were wild-looking, worse than I'd ever seen them. He glanced over at Dani and gave her a sharp look. I saw her start to say something, then stop, then drop her gaze to her lap. He stared at her for two long seconds, then turned back to me.

"Look, Nevers, I just want you to know I didn't believe all that bullshit about you being only interested in the money part of this film. You're too smart for that," he said.

"Okay." I nodded. I could see he was on a short fuse. I didn't know how short or what I should expect if he blew.

"You've got to help me," he insisted.

"How?" I looked at him quizzically.

"With Pope. Do you know why he wants to cut my script?"

"To save money."

"No, so he can insert twenty-five minutes of sex," Kessler spat. "He wants to take out twenty-five minutes of action and put in twenty-five minutes of tits and ass. You've got to stop him. You've got to," Kessler insisted as he ran his hands through his hair.

"I'm an investor, not a moviemaker," I started to explain, but he jumped right back in.

"Then, you're smart enough to know that tits and ass don't sell movies. Look, you've got to promise me you'll talk to Pope. You've got to, or we're all screwed."

I figured the fastest way to get rid of him was to

agree to speak to Pope. So I did. He seemed somewhat relieved but far from calmed down.

The whole piece of business with Kessler, from the time he first knocked on the door to the time he was gone, took no more than seven minutes. But something happened during those seven minutes that I didn't quite understand. I tried to laugh off Kessler's visit, but Dani's mood had changed. She was on edge. I asked her what was the matter, but she said she was okay. She wasn't okay. She threw up some sort of barrier between us, and before I could sit down again, she was on her feet and looking for her coat.

"I guess I'm really not ready to be with people tonight," she said coolly.

She said she thought it would be better if she went back to her place and spent the night. I started to ask her again what was wrong, but she gave me a cutting look, so I backed off. She even turned down my offer to give her a ride home and insisted on taking a taxi.

There was nothing I could do but roll with the punches.

Chapter Fifteen

The next day I spent the morning and better part of the afternoon looking after business at the hydroponics plant. Late in the afternoon I drove out to Kleinberg. I'd called in the morning to make an appointment with Pope. I'd promised Kessler I'd have a talk with Pope. It was also a good excuse to go out to the studio on the off chance I might run into Dani. I still hadn't figured that one out. I knew enough to keep my distance. On the other hand, sometimes the people who push you away the hardest are the ones who need you the most. I just wanted to be in range if she felt like talking. It wouldn't have done my ego any harm if, when she felt like talking, she wanted to do it with me.

I found Pope in his office going over head sheets of male actors. He held up a couple of pictures for me to see, and asked what I thought of them. They looked like your typical young Hollywood leading man, but what did I know.

I told Pope about the confrontation with Kessler the previous evening. Pope just laughed.

"I'm not crazy," he told me. "I'm not trying to shoot *Deep Throat* with Nazis. All I'm trying to do is put a little feeling into the picture, a little warmth."

"Twenty-five minutes of sex sounds like enough warmth to heat Alaska," I said, trying to humor him.

"More like five minutes total, spread out in thirty-second spots throughout the film. And nothing hardcore," he assured me. "Real stuff like Fonda and Voigt in *Coming Home*. You can't sucker the audiences in anymore to see a blowjob, but you can reach them with hardcore realism. The kids who go to movies are smart. They want it real. They want to be able to smell what's going on."

What Pope said made sense. I had no way of knowing whether he was telling the truth about his own intentions or shining me on. I was getting to the point where I really didn't care. I was quickly getting tired of the movie business. I'd fulfilled my promise to Kessler. Pope asked me to stick around and go through head sheets with him. I declined. My gut feeling was to get out of there and get as far away from this guy and his business as possible.

When I got back to my car I had a surprise waiting for me. Dani was sitting on the passenger side on the front seat. I'd walked by the office where she worked earlier but her desk was empty. I hadn't bothered to ask anybody if she was there or not.

I got in the car beside her, and she just smiled.

"You mad at me for last night?" she asked.

"No." I shook my head.

"No, I didn't think you would be," she said, moving closer to me and leaning her head on my shoulder. "Your place," she added, then fell silent. It was like a replay of the night before. Neither of us spoke, but there was a nice feeling in the air. For my part, I didn't need any explanations. I was happy she was back.

This time when we got to my place we didn't even bother with the drinks or music. We were in my bed in less than two minutes.

"I'm going to make it up to you for last night," was all she said. We went at each other with the hunger of sharks and the playfulness of dolphins. In one of my more lucid moments that evening, I realized I had never been made love to like that before in my life. The wait for this one had been worth every minute. When we finally fell asleep from sheer exhaustion, we were like two wet beavers, pressed so tightly together we were sharing the same skin.

The first rays of light were just coming through the

curtains when I woke up. For a moment I felt disoriented, like something was wrong. Then I realized I was alone. I looked at my clock. It was six thirty. I realized she'd slipped out of the apartment sometime before that. I felt colder than I should have felt, waking up in bed alone. I got up and put on my clothes and went for a long walk. She hadn't left a note. She hadn't said anything about leaving early. Maybe she'd tried to wake me. I had slept through similar situations before. I tried not to think too much about it or make too much out of what was probably nothing. On the other hand, the night before she'd bolted after seeing Kessler. I hadn't sorted that one out yet.

By the time I got back to the hotel and had had breakfast, I'd made up my mind that everything was fine. The best thing for me to do was to just go about my business. I finished the morning paper and headed up to my rooms.

My phone was ringing when I got there. I couldn't help hoping it was Dani. It wasn't. It was Pope, sounding like the cat who just ate the goldfish. He was calling to invite me to a party that night at his house to announce the new male lead for the film.

"I've signed someone really special," he said.

"Who?" I asked out of politeness.

"You'll just have to come to the party if you want to find out," he insisted.

"I'm not sure I can make it," I told him. "Why don't you just let me know now, just in case I can't show up."

"If you don't come tonight, you'll have to read about it in the papers," Pope said slyly.

"So, I'll read it in the papers. Thanks for the invite. I'll be there if I can," I said, hanging up. I wasn't in the mood for long conversations or guessing games. The bottom line was that I didn't need to know who was in the picture until the day after or the day after that, if ever. I was a minor investor, I reminded myself. I'd been acting more like a groupie in the last few weeks, and I was beginning to get on my own nerves.

I drove out to Ajax and lost myself in projections

of annual tomato yields per square foot of manufacturing space. I had no intention of going to the party, and I wouldn't have if I hadn't gotten the one call that could change my mind.

Dani called about three fifteen. She wanted to know if I was going to the party, and if I was, could I pick her up. When I thought about it, I really didn't have anything better to do, so I agreed to pick her up at seven.

A security guard was still posted outside the door which led to the double suite Dani shared with Catherine at the Airport Motor Inn. The guard looked up briefly at me when I knocked on the door, then went back to reading his magazine.

Dani opened the door and invited me in. She was wearing a black evening gown that hung on her like a second skin.

She closed the door behind us and offered me a drink before we left for the party. Catherine had gone straight from the studio to Pope's place. We were alone. I was still standing up when she brought me my drink.

"I guess you must think it was kind of strange of me to up and leave you this morning without saying good-bye," she said with a half smile on her face.

I tried to shrug it off as not important. I guess she could tell that it had bothered me, if only slightly. She laughed.

"At least I know you care," she said, coming up to me and giving me a warm kiss. "I'm coming onto my period in a day or two, and I get kind of crazy around this time every month," she said by way of explanation. What she did next didn't need any explanation. She stepped back, put her drink down, turned her back, and pulled her gown off over her head. She was naked underneath. She bent down, picked up her dress, and covered the front of her body before she turned around to face me. I was still standing there with my drink in my hand, and fully dressed. But not for long. I picked her up and carried her to the bed where we both agreed the party could wait.

I was in favor of canceling out on the party altogether, but Dani insisted we go. She'd promised she'd show up. Dani had a funny sense of loyalty to Catherine that, in a strange way, I liked. When people treat their friends well, they're likely to treat you well too if they're your friend.

We got dressed and arrived at the party about nine thirty. There were several security guards posted outside. They were the same guards from the studio, so they waved us inside.

There were about forty people in the apartment when we arrived. I spotted Pope, Catherine, Kessler, and Catherine's drama coach right away. About half the others were people who worked at the studio or worked for the media. The rest I figured were friends or friends of friends. Movie parties had a way of bringing out a certain regular crowd in the city. The only one who I expected to see but didn't was Bridges. But two of his young bimbos were there. They appeared to be a couple. They spent all their time dancing together cheek to cheek or holding hands in the corner and giggling and whispering into each other's ears.

I told Pope as soon as I saw him that I hoped he'd get his announcement over with, so we could all leave. He thought I was joking and laughed it off.

"Soon," he said, slapping me on the back. "I just want to wait a few more minutes."

I didn't ask him for what. I really didn't care. As far as I was concerned, as soon as Dani was through paying her respects we'd leave.

She was hanging pretty close to Catherine. Catherine told us out of earshot that Pope had been a real bastard to her all day. He had been teasing her about the new lead but wouldn't tell her who it was.

"And I'm the one who has to play opposite," she said nervously, twirling a half empty wineglass in her hand. "I don't think I'm going to be able to make it through the rest of the night on the second half of this glass. I wish the bastard would hurry up."

We didn't have much longer to wait. Less than a minute later, Pope stopped the music and called us

72

around him. Dani and I moved with Catherine to the front of the circle of people who ringed Pope. He stood up on a chair.

"I was hoping he would have been able to show up by now," Pope said, presumably referring to the new male lead, "but obviously he hasn't made it as yet. I know you've all been waiting patiently to hear who will play the part opposite Catherine St. Catherine. I won't keep you waiting any longer. After careful consideration, I have made what I believe to be one of the most brilliant choices in modern filmmaking. I am certain that he will contribute immeasurably to the success of the film. Many of you know him personally. The rest of you have seen his work on television or in the theater. I am sure you have been as impressed as I have been. I am delighted to announce that at nine o'clock today we signed the final agreements with Clem Dunkin to play the lead in the film *Crash,* which will begin shooting in ten days' time."

The name Clem Dunkin was greeted with a stunned silence by the party guests. Several of the media people quietly broke away from the crowd and went to make their phone calls to their respective papers. The others simply looked from one to the other with blank expressions on their faces. Pope ignored the reaction, got down from the chair, and turned the music back on.

Catherine was the first to speak. She walked to the bar, downed the last half of the glass in her hand, and picked up a second glass.

"Well, let's celebrate," she said, downing the second glass in one gulp. The others began milling about the room talking quietly in small groups. The entire room was in a state of shock.

I picked up on bits and pieces of conversation while Dani hung close to Catherine and tried to keep her off the bottle.

Clem Dunkin was a virtual unknown outside of the city. He was well known as a local stage performer and had been a regular on the Bobby Vinton show where he did a pratfall routine, but he'd never been in a film. I'd seen him two or three times on stage and a couple of times on TV. He was strikingly good-looking and likable enough. He was one of those people who is constantly doing some sort of routine for a laugh. He usually got laughs. But that didn't necessarily make him star quality in a blockbuster film, especially a film that was supposed to be about as funny as smallpox.

Pope let the thinly veiled barbs about Clem Dunkin run off his back. "Clem is an excellent performer. I think he'll add a dimension that no other actor could add to the part," Pope explained to one of the city's top movie critics. "He'll play well against Catherine."

Kessler brushed by me on his way to the door.

"I told you he was going to screw us," Kessler said as he went by me. I just nodded.

Little jokes started to pop up around the room that Pope had gone crazy or broke or both. Then, someone got the bright idea that Pope was putting them on. Everyone wanted to believe that so badly that a kind of gaiety was coming back into the room when Clem Dunkin showed up.

He was all smiles. With a couple of exceptions, everybody crowded around him and congratulated him. I didn't because I didn't know the guy from Adam. Catherine didn't. She didn't seem particularly happy and was hitting the sauce again. And Dani didn't because she was trying to wean Catherine away from the bottle.

Dunkin managed one magnificent fall on his way to meet Pope, and it took everybody's breath away. He got up and apologized for his clumsiness. He gave Pope a big hug and kiss, then announced to the crowd that he was going to be concentrating on more serious roles.

"A good actor has to be able to get more than laughs," he told the party. As he talked he leaned against the buffet table for support. He set his right arm on the table behind him and managed to dunk his arm midway to the elbow in the punch bowl.

The room exploded in laughter. The only one who didn't seem to think any of it was amusing was Catherine.

"Asshole," I heard her mutter under her breath as she stared in the general direction of Pope and Clem

Dunkin. Clem was doing a very funny routine, a fake magic act with jokes à la Steve Martin.

Catherine was in no mood to be entertained. She decided to leave. She asked Dani to go with her. Dani agreed. I offered to drive them, but Catherine insisted on calling a cab. I was able to talk briefly with Dani before the cab arrived.

I figured Catherine was upset about Dunkin's ability to make it in the film. I was wrong. Dunkin's acting ability had nothing to do with Catherine's black mood.

"I don't know if I should be telling you this," Dani explained, "but I feel like I owe you some kind of explanation, so you don't think I'm screwing you around."

"You don't need to explain yourself, Dani. I trust you," I told her.

"Then, let's just say it's for me. I don't think I can handle it all by myself anymore," she began. "You're not going to believe this, but Catherine's been seeing Clem Dunkin secretly on the side for about a year."

"Is she in love with him?" I asked. It was a pretty banal response, but I couldn't think of anything else to say.

"I don't know. I don't think Catherine knows."

"What about Pope? Does he know about the affair?"

"I would have said no, up until tonight. Catherine and Clem were very discreet. I don't see how anyone could have found out. But now, I just don't know."

Just then, the cab buzzed from downstairs. Catherine put on her coat and left first. Dani kissed me and said if things settled down, she'd try to make it over to my place that night. She already had a spare key from the night before the siege, so she could let herself in.

"Not to worry," she said, kissing me warmly a second time, then headed down the hall after her friend.

Suddenly, I was looking at things from a very different point of view. Was this some sort of monumental coincidence about Pope choosing Catherine's other lover to star in the picture opposite her? Or did he know? Was this some bizarre twist of perversion on his part, throwing Catherine and Clem Dunkin together? Whatever

Pope's intentions or innocence, it was going to weigh heavily on Catherine's shoulders. That frail psyche was already standing on the edge.

Catherine's affair had left a sour taste in my mouth. Not because I approved or disapproved, but because I sensed it was just one of a number of skeletons that were going to be popping out of the closet before the film was completed.

I buttonholed Pope before I left and started to pump him on why he'd made the decision to go with Clem Dunkin instead of a bankable name. Pope tried to fancy-step his way out of my reach but I boxed him into a corner and demanded a straight answer.

"If you really want to know, I'll tell you," he said in a whisper, so no one could overhear us.

"Just tell it to me straight. No bullshit."

What he laid out for me I didn't like one damned bit. He said he'd been forced to change the script and go for an unknown because they were expecting to run into a serious deficit.

"I thought you said the five million was enough," I reminded him.

"What five million?" He looked at me as if I was dumb or something. "We'll be lucky if we can get our hands on two."

I looked at him askance. "But I saw the figures. There's five point two million in commitments as of ten days ago. Now, what exactly are you trying to tell me."

"I'm telling you what Bridges told me. That's all I know and it's more than I want to know. If you have any more questions, ask him," he said bitterly. "Now if you'll excuse me, I'm going to have a nice time."

Pope walked away from me and returned to the crowd, smiling and laughing as though he had completely blanked out everything he just told me.

I left right afterward. I didn't sleep much that night. Dani didn't make it over either.

Chapter Sixteen

I was at Bridges's office by eight thirty. He was already there.

He didn't shake my hand or even bother to get up from his desk. He just looked at me and shook his head. "We got a few problems. We'll work them out," he said matter-of-factly.

"How bad is it?" I demanded.

"That depends on whether you're an optimist or a pessimist," he said, handing me a sheet of paper. "Read this. It just came in over the facs."

I looked at the piece of paper he had handed me. It was a sheet of Unico Industries letterhead. There was a dateline on the page for a nine o'clock release that morning. It was a terse press release announcing that Unico Industries was selling National Pictures to the Norfo Corporation of Cincinnati for three hundred million dollars in cash and stock.

On the surface it didn't look like much. One conglomerate selling a piece of the pie to another conglomerate, but I'd been around long enough to be able to read between the lines. I suspected the worst. But I wanted to hear it from Bridges's mouth.

"They've frozen our deal on *Crash* until the sale goes through to Norfo," he said.

"How long do you figure it might stay frozen?"

"At least for ninety days while the two companies work through the shareholder and Security and Exchange approvals, and then maybe forever. Norfo wants to get out of the picture financing business and concentrate on distribution," he explained. "In any case, we'd be out of business if we tried to wait them out."

"How long have you known about this?" I asked.

"I got the first signals about eight days ago. Four days ago, I knew for sure."

"Why didn't you tell me?"

"Tell you what? That two of the biggest companies in the world were selling off our golden goose? What were you going to do about it?"

I nodded. He was right. It was just one of those wild cards that seemed to pop up whenever anything was so perfect you just couldn't lose.

"So we're down two million dollars," I said, mentally writing off the two million the production had been counting on from National Pictures.

"Four million," he corrected me.

"Four million?" I asked, not wanting to believe I was hearing right.

"Do you want it straight or do you want it nice?" he asked me.

"Give it to me straight," I said. "And slowly so I don't miss anything."

"The two million from the government was contingent on the National Pictures' deal. Even if we come up with another two million, the government money's no longer a sure thing."

"It never was, was it?"

"We were negotiating in good faith. We had a good product and we had a good chance."

"Well, we still have a million to work with," I said. "That should buy us some time."

I didn't like the way Bridges was looking at me. He swallowed hard. "That's all gone, too, Billy," he informed me.

I looked at him dumbly. "How the hell could it be all gone?"

"Pre-production. We've tied up the studio at Kleinberg for two weeks. And then there's the nasty little bit of business with St. Catherine and Reverend Smith. Don't think that didn't cost plenty. Why, the security guards alone have eaten up a hundred and thirty thousand. Did you think they were working for free?"

Bridges wasn't finished yet with the bad news. There was some chance we could still pull the picture off. The story was set. The studio was booked, and we could at least count on some international box office on the basis of Catherine St. Catherine. The fly in the ointment was Kessler and the script.

Bridges's production company didn't own the film rights to Kessler's story. It owned an option on the story. Kessler had been paid only twenty thousand for a one-year option that was going to run out in eighteen days.

"How much is that going to cost?" I asked.

"Another hundred thousand," Bridges explained.

Bridges didn't have the hundred thousand. He didn't even have ten thousand.

"The shit should hit the fan in about three days when the checks start bouncing," he mused.

"Don't you have any money of your own that you can bridge the deal with?" I asked.

He looked at me like I was a lunatic. "I put up all the money I had to keep this thing floating for six months before I got those dentists from Winnipeg on board."

It was hard for me to imagine that Bridges didn't have some stashed somewhere after three hundred movies.

"You make money on the good ones and you sink it back on the dogs," he explained. "The only way you come out ahead is if you have some really big winners and some very smart accountants who know how to beat the tax men. I had my share of winners, but never the really big ones that you count on to get you over the top. As for accountants, I've had them both smart and crooked. Those bastards took everything the tax boys didn't take," he said, then pointed to his mouth and smiled broadly, exposing the missing teeth. "If I had any money, don't you think I'd have these holes in my head plugged up?"

I nodded. I wanted to be mad at the guy, but I just couldn't find it in my heart to hate him, or even for that matter dislike him. I made a mental note that if I ever shook his hand again, I'd count my fingers afterward.

Chapter Seventeen

"Can we do it for less than the five million?" I asked.

"Films are a funny business, my man. It's one of the few things in this world for which the customer pays the same price regardless of the cost. Doesn't matter if it costs a million or a hundred million to make. The trick about making money in this business is to give the customer something that enough of them will want to plunk down their dollars to see. In my opinion, our only hope in hell of getting those people to want to see this picture would be to spend the full five million above what's been spent to date. Without it, we just won't have the production values and quality to make a picture of this scope work."

Maybe the smartest thing I could have done was walk out that door and leave Bridges to his own misery. There was a good chance I'd never see my money again. Then, I really wasn't hurting with the income from the hydroponics plant coming on stream in six or seven months. I wasn't in a hot cash position, but then I wasn't expecting any major expenses; so I'd manage somehow.

In the end, it wasn't the money that made up my mind. It was the challenge. Sure, I was looking after my own investments, but that was only part of it. The biggest part was not wanting to admit I'd been taken to the cleaners with my eyes wide open. I guess you could call it personal pride.

With National Pictures out of the deal and the government still negotiating, I was the largest single investor in the picture. There was still a decent chance, according to Bridges, that we'd be able to secure the two million from the government. That still left three million to be raised privately—two million to replace the National money and a million more to make up for what had already been spent in pre-production costs.

We decided to split up the workload. Since Bridges was already negotiating with the government, he'd stick to that and try to push through the mountain of paper work necessary to close that part of the deal. I would work the private money.

I took on the title of executive producer. It wasn't meant to be an honorary degree. I'd insisted from the start that I be kept informed of everything. That included every move that Bridges made, every thought that he thought, even everything he didn't think was worth thinking about. I was still flying by the seat of my pants. I figured I'd need every scrap of input if I was going to pull this one out of the nosedive it was in.

My very first job was to raise the hundred thousand dollars to exercise the option on Kessler's story. Without the story, there wasn't any movie. We could kiss everything good-bye. I figured raising the hundred thousand would be a piece of cake. I couldn't have been more wrong.

Trying to raise money for the film was a little like trying to peddle contraceptives in an old-age home. I didn't have any trouble finding people who were interested. I found a dozen in the first three days alone who wanted to have dinner with Catherine St. Catherine, or if not her, then any blond, blue-eyed young thing I could lay my hands on, but no one wanted to touch their wallets. Not for a hundred thousand, not for ten thousand, not for a single dime.

I tried every bank, trust company, investment house, and venture capital group I could think of. I worked through my personal list of friends, acquaintances, and people I knew who didn't necessarily like me but were big spenders. I would have had more luck trying to raise the dead. Word was out on the street that National Pictures was out of the deal. Nobody wanted to be the first one back in. I started to get the feeling that maybe I'd bought a one-way ticket on the *Titanic*. And it wasn't just the money part of the deal that was turning sour.

Bridges, bless his heart, had managed to keep the public relations machinery well oiled. Word was out on the street that we were broke all right, but none of the media boys had heard about it yet. The entertainment section of every daily in the city carried some juicy bit on the film, Catherine St. Catherine, Clem Dunkin, or Lazlo Pope. Both Bridges, as producer, and I, as executive producer, were mentioned or quoted frequently. In one way, all the publicity was good. It gave us a high profile. In another way, it was bad because slowly the truth about our financial situation began to leak out.

The first real bad weather came one afternoon when I was having lunch with Meyer Bigelow, an old friend and president of the Royal Canadian Trust Company. We had gone to his private club, the Adelaide House, where I was trying to explain why I thought the film deal was worth investing in. He'd already turned me down corporately, but I figured he might be good for fifty or a hundred thou on his own. If I could get him in, I'd have a chance of possibly talking a few of his buddies to go in. In that dining room for lunch alone, there was easily six hundred million dollars in personal assets among the thirty-odd members who had shown up that day. Every one of them sat on at least two boards of the top hundred largest corporations in the country. I could have raised a quick quarter of a million just selling the furniture in that place.

Meyer Bigelow didn't owe me. But he liked me, and that counted for something. I'd handled a part of his stock portfolio when I was still in the brokerage business. People like Meyer, who handle billions of other people's money so well, are notorious for handling their own money poorly. Meyer did all right with me. I added fifty percent to his portfolio in a little over twenty-six months, then advised him to get out and buy gold when it was still under a hundred dollars an ounce. He did and told me later he'd made a very nice gain.

I might have had a reasonable chance selling Meyer on the film deal if I hadn't left word at the office where I could be reached in an emergency.

The emergency turned out to be Harold D. Kessler. He came in person to bring his own very special brand of bad news. He'd covered big business at one time, so it wasn't too hard for him to bluff his way into the dining room of the Adelaide House.

He was dressed in a jacket and tie to conform to the dress standards, but I knew from the look in his eyes he hadn't come to eat. My first instinct was to jump up and run him the hell out of there before he opened his mouth. But he was already shouting before I could move.

"I'll see that you don't raise one damned penny," he said, screaming at me hysterically. "I'll stop it before I'll see it ruined."

I was on my feet, but it was already too late. Kessler, still ranting about how the movie was his and that Bridges and I were destroying it, tipped over my table and sent poor Meyer Bigelow to the floor. I thought he was hurt. I stooped down to see if he was okay. He assured me he was all right. By the time I was on my feet again, Kessler had managed to dump three more tables before he was grabbed by two burly waiters who carried him kicking and screaming from the room.

I had only to look around the room to know I was washed up. The president of the country's largest bank was wearing his chateaubriand in his lap. The chairman of the second largest retail chain in the east was picking salad out of his toupee.

Meyer Bigelow called me later in the afternoon and confided to me that he hadn't enjoyed himself so much in years, but that it was out of the question for him to invest after what had happened. Even if he thought it was a good idea, he'd lose too much face among his own colleagues. He said he was sorry and hung up.

The Adelaide House had no interest in pressing

charges, so Kessler went scott free. I kept a sharp eye out for the rat. I was in the mood to skin him.

Bridges was running into trouble, too.

"I just don't know what's wrong," he confided to me. "The doors keep slamming shut."

Pope had originally introduced the British-born Bridges to government circles. In his early days at the CBC, Pope had worked with a number of people who had become influential senior bureaucrats in the federal government. The most influential of all was the Minister of Economic Development, Malcolm Hennessey Devoir. Devoir, the product of two establishment families—one Montreal-French and the other Toronto-English-Irish—was looked on as an institution. Handsome almost to the point of being beautiful, Devoir had gone to work for the CBC, after graduating with high honors from Osgoode Hall Law School.

His background plus his good looks which included a full head of hair that had gone a premature silvery gray before his twenty-fourth birthday, earning him the nickname "The Silver Fox" had made him a highly popular television personality. He had had his own talk show for two years and was on the national news for another two. He had been offered several contracts in New York but turned them all down. He had been born to privilege, with all of Canada as his private fiefdom. Despite the bad weather and long winters, he knew before he could speak, when he was only able to listen, that he could be Prime Minister of Canada one day if he played his cards right.

After his stint with the CBC, which established him as a household word and popular personality, he took up law, championing a number of popular liberal causes and making himself visible within the cultural world by becoming a prime fund raiser for the theater, opera, and ballet. He spent several years working in the family corporation, which was a major force in pulp and paper and metal fabrication.

To the surprise of no one, he left the family business, put his holdings in a blind trust, and ran on the

Liberal ticket for Parliament and easily won a seat as a member of the House, representing the old-money district of Rosedale.

By that time he had married the equally spectacular Betty Harlen McDouglas, of McDouglas Industries, one one of the country's larger newspaper empires, which included in its holdings the *Toronto News.*

Devoir had held a number of cabinet positions, the latest of which was the Economic Development portfolio. The Department of Economic Development was a key department as a result of the ongoing French-English split in the country. Its mandate was to keep the country together through economic development. Interestingly the department had been reorganized to include the old Department of Cultural Affairs, and with it had come all the funding power for the arts and, in particular, films. The government regarded culture as a key area in the separatism fight and had brought it under the fold of the Economic Development Department in order to give it buying power. One of the department's most visible activities was the creation of employment through make-work jobs. More than a hundred million dollars had already been poured into new galleries and theaters, arts activities, and such pseudo-art ventures as mural painting on the walls of buildings in depressed areas, local arts and crafts workshops, and, of course, movies. They were all highly visible ventures that people could see and touch. These kinds of projects not only appealed to the liberal and more radical youth but also employed a great deal of manpower in the work itself and in the actual operation of the new government-funded theater groups and art camps.

The government had feverishly been trying to maintain these activities despite the fact that heavy spending in these non-wealth-producing ventures, coupled with some miserably bad economic policies for industry, had driven nearly ten percent of the manufacturing sector out of the country. These factories had closed and taken their jobs with them, driving the unemployment figures up to twelve percent.

There was no doubt that the government was in trouble. The dollar bought only fifty-two cents of what it had bought seven years before. The inflation rate was chugging along at sixteen percent and rising. As the numbers got worse, the anglophone-francophone war escalated. There was more hate and more people who wanted to see the country chopped up.

More and more of the votes were going to separatist groups who favored independence for the western provinces or Quebec. Even Ontario and the Atlantic provinces had elected members to the federal Parliament who favored negotiated separation from Canada. One group in British Columbia claimed that it had already made application to join the United States.

Devoir's party was still managing to hold the country together but from a minority position. It had maintained its power by playing the splinter groups off against each other, essentially by giving the province that cried the loudest the biggest piece of the federal tax revenues. The more it gave away, the further it fell into debt. The government was reduced to borrowing more and more money on foreign markets to pay for essentials like its armed forces. What it couldn't borrow, it squeezed out of the middle class by raising taxes to the extent that the middle class was becoming an endangered species.

The bad economic climate had existed for a number of years. Through it all, the government had maintained the film incentives and had, in fact, increased funding in this area, because the program was popular, movies were highly visible and entertaining and kept people off the streets, and the money stayed in the country.

But suddenly the government seemed to be reversing its policy. Devoir wouldn't even answer Bridges's phone calls.

"I can't tell if they're closing down the film financing or whether they've blackballed our film," Bridges told me despondently. "Every time I call, they keep telling me he's busy."

"Have you tried Pope? He should be able to get

through at least to see if Devoir's really busy or just giving us the brush-off."

"I didn't want to tell you this," he said, "but Pope's disappeared."

Chapter Eighteen

Pope had vanished and had taken Catherine St. Catherine with him. We did find a note he'd left in the top right-hand drawer of his desk addressed to Bridges. It said simply: "Catherine and I have gone for a few days. Will return when rested. Lazlo."

It was definitely his writing and his signature. Bridges thought it might be foul play, but there was no real indication that we should get the police involved, at least not yet.

We started calling around. Apparently he'd told no one where he was going or even that he was going at all. The cash deposit with the security agency had been eaten up three days before. They'd taken all their guards off the job, so they were no help. There hadn't been any sign of the Flock of God people, so we were likely in the clear on that one.

Even Dani didn't know Catherine was gone. Dani had been spending almost all her time with me. She was about the only good thing that had come out of the movie deal.

She allayed my fears about the possibility that something bad might have happened to Pope or Catherine.

"Not to worry," she assured me. "They have a knack for disappearing whenever there's a hiatus."

"Any idea where they might be?" I asked.

"Montreal, Niagara Falls, Kingston, Buffalo, some tiny motel on the lake shore, anywhere within a hard day's drive. They never tell anyone and never go to the same place twice."

"How long do these little jaunts usually last?"

"Two or three days, a week sometimes. Just as long as Lazlo feels it won't hurt the film. He says he has a sixth sense about knowing when the money's going to show up and things are going to start rolling again."

We were in pretty bad shape. No doubt about it. In hindsight, maybe the best thing I could have done was take a walk myself. Most of the people at the studio had abandoned ship once the money ran out to pay their salaries. A few of the more desperate ones were hanging in on deferred salaries and promises, hoping that something might show up to help pay the rent. It was a pretty depressed group.

Pope's disappearance was just another letdown to the morale. Worse, we were losing precious time working through the government bureaucracy. I had enough to do without having to call every motel in a four-hundred-mile radius. Bridges, Dani, and I worked the phones until midnight before calling it quits. Dani and I went back to my place to sleep, both of us mentally and physically wiped out. I had a lot more on my mind than just finding Pope.

I'd made up my mind I was going to raise the hundred thousand one way or the other. Since I had been turned down by just about every *other* I knew, it was plain that I'd have to put my own neck on the line. Again.

I was going to have to negotiate a personal loan against my future income from the hydroponics plant. I figured I needed a hundred and fifty thousand dollars—a hundred to pay off Kessler and an extra fifty to give me enough time to raise the rest of the five million we'd need to get the picture made.

"You believe in it that much?" Dani asked, playing the devil's advocate.

"It's a solid deal," I repeated for the umpteenth time, as much for my sake as hers. "Once I can convince a few people that I'm behind it all the way, they'll come around."

"Don't you think it might be better to cut your losses and walk away?" she asked. "You'd have a wonderful tax advantage as is."

"If I lost another hundred and fifty thousand, I'd be in tax heaven," I tried to joke. Actually, I'd be a long way down and would be out a lot of hard-earned money. "I have to see this one through."

I was getting myself in over my head. No doubt about it. But I'd been there before with worse odds. The one thing I was sure of, there was no way of winning without playing.

I'd made an appointment with my bank manager for nine o'clock the next morning. It was going to be a tough fight convincing him to cut loose a hundred and fifty thousand against my future earnings in the vegetable factory, but I figured I could do it if I set my mind to it.

I might have if I'd ever made it to that appointment, but I didn't.

The phone rang just before eight that morning. If I'd gone out the door just a few minutes earlier I might have made it to the bank.

I picked up the phone, wondering who would be calling that early in the morning. Dani was still asleep in the other room. It was Jane Willson.

"Billy, can you come to Ajax right away?" she asked. She sounded calm enough but there was something slightly off in her voice.

"What's wrong?" I asked. Something had to be or she wouldn't be asking me to come out there. She barely tolerated me on the site at the best of times. She was good-natured but nevertheless made no bones about the fact that she'd just as soon not have me hanging around.

"We've had some trouble. I'd rather not go into the details on the phone."

"Can it wait a few hours?" I asked, hoping against hope it wasn't so urgent that I'd be unable to make my nine o'clock.

"Billy, please," she pleaded with me. She started to say more but her voice cracked.

"I'm on my way," I assured her and hung up.

I drove as fast as I could, but I'd hit the 401 right

in the middle of rush hour when it turns into one of the world's longest parking lots. I wondered if I should have called the police. I figured Jane would have done that immediately if she thought it necessary. She was one of the most competent managers I'd ever met. This somewhat relieved my anxiety.

When I arrived, everything looked more or less normal. There were no police cars in sight. The parking lot was filled with cars belonging to the construction crew. Nothing abnormal about that. If they hadn't been there, I might have started to worry.

Even Gino's Snack Wagon was parked near the entrance like it normally was at that time of the day. There were a few more workers around the snack wagon than usual but I only noticed that because I was looking for something. Anything. I didn't know what yet. I made a mental note that no one would make eye contact with me as I headed toward the entrance of the plant.

There I saw the first signs of what had been done. The glass in the double doors lay all about the entrance and the metal frames were bowed. That was only the beginning.

The inside of the factory looked like it had been hit with a bomb. Actually, several bombs. The irrigation systems had been blown from their moorings and were scattered about like great twisted snakes. The concrete growing troughs had been reduced to fist-sized piles of rubble. The lighting and electrical work had been ripped from the ceiling and cut to scrap lengths. The auxillary generators had been turned into two twisted piles of metal junk.

Most of the construction crew were standing about in small groups talking among themselves. Jane walked slowly around the plant floor with her clipboard, kicking through the piles of rubble with the toe of her right shoe.

As I walked toward her, I could see her mouth was set hard, her lips were thin lines across her face. She looked up when I approached her, but there was only partial recognition in her eyes, like she was in shock. I took her by the arm and led her out of sight and hearing of the others. The office was a wreck, with papers and files blown all about the room, but at least it still had a door that closed. I walked Jane inside and shut the door behind us.

"Was anyone hurt?" I asked.

"No, there wasn't anyone here," she said with just a little too much composure.

"What about security?"

"They drove through at six A.M. and everything was clear. I was the first one here at seven thirty. It must have happened in between."

"Have you called the police?"

"Yes, of course. They sent two detectives who looked around and said they'd be back later. That was more than an hour ago. The insurance agent said he'd be here by eleven." She smiled broadly and gave a hearty little laugh before continuing. "Now, how do you suggest we handle the P.R.?"

That smile and little laugh were her last efforts to keep up the tough front. Underneath that tough facade she was broken-hearted. I watched the lines of her face change, the lips quiver, and then heard the almost inaudible moan that came from deep inside just before the dam broke. A moment later she was clinging to me and sobbing uncontrollably. I let her cry herself out, then I knew she was okay. But I couldn't help hating whoever had made her go through that pain. She'd never be all-the-way better. I knew the insurance would pay to rebuild, but it could never pay for her lost time or for the horror of seeing her efforts so utterly destroyed. It would always be there in the back of her mind that maybe someone, someday might do this to her again. Maybe she wouldn't think about it consciously, but it would be there. That's how it is with bad things.

I stayed the rest of the day while Jane assessed the damage. I tried to get her to take the day off, but of course she insisted on staying. It was probably the best thing for her. She was set on rebuilding right away.

The police arson squad showed up later that morning and confirmed that dynamite had caused most of the damage. Not one blast, but a number of small blasts placed strategically in just the right spots. Considering the time element, there were probably a number of people involved. Some cut what couldn't be blown up, while the others set the charges to go off like a series of Chinese firecrackers, doing maximum damage but exploding one charge at a time to reduce the noise factor. Most of the plants in the immediate area were empty at night and those few people who could be found, who might have heard something, said they hadn't heard a thing. No one could be found who had noticed anything or anyone unusual in the area either.

Whoever had done it knew exactly what they were doing. The damage was total. The only thing left was the shell of the building itself.

The insurance would pay the replacement costs of the building, but there was no way we'd make up for the lost revenues from the vegetable sales. I couldn't count on any money for at least a year and a half, and then there was no guarantee that Anglo-American, the grocery wholesaler, would honor the agreement after the delay. There was an outside chance I had just lost everything. In any case I'd lost the bargaining power to raise the hundred and fifty thousand from the bank. What little cash I had on hand went to pay for full-time security at the plant site in case the mad bombers decided to come back to blow the building down.

Driving back to the city, I listened to the account of the bombing over the radio. It had broken about an hour before. Jane and I both left before the reporters started to arrive. The news commentator said that, so far, the police had no suspects. They may not have had any, but I knew who had done it. There was no question in my mind.

Chapter Nineteen

When I got back to the hotel, Dani handed me an envelope. It was marked "Special Delivery."

"It arrived about forty minutes ago," she said. "I tried to reach you at Ajax but you'd already left."

I opened the envelope. It contained a single sheet of paper. The letters had been cut from newspapers and magazines and pasted onto the sheet. There was no salutation. The text read:

"God has demanded a rain of fire on the head of he who permits pornography and the growing of food by unnatural means."

Underneath was the signature. An octagon with a cross inside and two crossed shepherd's staffs behind it. The signature only confirmed my worst fears. It was the symbol of the Flock of God cult. We had all seen it enough times during the siege to be sure it was theirs. It was possible that it might have been a forged note, but the bombing itself had all the earmarks of the way they had signed their name in the past. They were known to be expert demolition technicians and had shown their skills within the Flock in the past. They also had a reputation for damaging property only. No one had ever been killed or physically injured in all the incidents.

It was possible that it could have been someone else. It crossed my mind that it could have been someone like Kessler, who had sworn publicly to stop the movie, but he would have had to employ a small army of experts to carry out the job. I didn't think he'd be able to raise the manpower or resources to pull off the job at Ajax.

At face value, the content of the note was almost humorous if it wasn't so creepy. I was the symbol of all that was bad about the movie because I was now the executive producer. Whether or not sex was good or bad, dirty or okay was an argument that had been going on a long, long time. I could see that the Flock people had a right to their point of view, although not a right to their means of protest. On the other side of the coin, it was hard for me to understand their reaction to the hydroponics plant. I had no doubt they had singled it out not only because it would cripple me financially, and thus presumably hurt the film, but because they also seemed to believe that growing food this way was somehow an act against God. It struck me as ironic that this means of growing things had been developed in India to feed the multitudes. The fertilizers were the exact same in chemical composition as those that made up natural fertilizers. A lot more food could be grown in a much smaller space, meaning that this method of production would probably be able to help stem the major world food shortages predicted for the next decade.

As far as I was concerned, if it was put to him, God would approve of hydroponics. As Dani put it, "The big question isn't Godly or unGodly. It's whether or not the world wants manure on its vegetables or wants to feed the masses."

I was just about to call the police when the phone rang. It was Lazlo Pope. He was downstairs with Catherine, had heard about the dynamiting at Ajax on his car radio, and wanted to come up to see me.

They both breezed into the room a minute later like two newlyweds. Obviously the little rest had done some good. But there was still a slight nervous air about them.

"I'm really sorry to hear about the plant," Pope said to me as casually as he could, while I mixed a round of drinks. Perrier for Pope and Catherine. Scotch, doubles, for Dani and me. They didn't know the truth yet. We did. I figured they'd switch soon enough.

Pope told us about a little inn they'd discovered in Aurora where they'd hid out for two days, just to get away from it all. Catherine told us all about the long walks they took at the crack of dawn, how they then went back to their room and slept until well past noon. Despite the chitchat, I could tell there was something else on their minds. I didn't suspect they'd hurried home because they'd got tired of their romantic retreat. I let them go on though, not really knowing how to tell them the truth. I had called the police about the note, and my old friend Lieutenant Hagen said they'd be right over. Dani had called Bridges and Clem Dunkin on my second phone, but they were out. She left word for them to call back as soon as they came in.

It was Catherine who finally popped the question. "You don't suppose the trouble at Ajax had anything to do with the film, do you?"

There wasn't much that I could say, so I handed her the note instead.

"This came in about an hour ago," I told her. "Hold it by the edges so if there are any fingerprints, they won't get smeared."

She held the page carefully and Pope looked over her shoulder and read it, too. Catherine let out a long, deep sigh. I almost had the feeling that she was somehow glad that she knew, instead of walking around with the weight of wondering.

"Are you sure it's real?" Pope said in a very subdued voice as Catherine handed the letter back.

"It's real," Catherine answered for me. All the color had gone out of her skin. She looked gray.

"Have you called the police?" Pope insisted.

"They're on their way," Dani informed him. "They'll be here any minute."

Pope and Catherine looked only slightly relieved. They both switched to Scotch before the police arrived.

Lieutenant Hagen showed up, accompanied by Lieutenant Brogan and two uniformed police. Brogan had dealt with the Flock of God siege and considered this an extension of his investigation. It was obvious that Hagen had just come along for the ride and as a courtesy to me. Brogan had a knack for offending.

It took him about three minutes of grilling to turn Catherine into a pile of tears. I was glad Hagen was there. It took both of us to keep Pope from taking a pop at Brogan for the way he was shaking up Catherine.

The interrogation turned up nothing, of course. None of us knew anything. Hagen did manage to get Brogan off our backs in just under an hour. I wasn't sorry to see him go. They left the two uniformed police with us as protection. One for Dani and me and the other for Catherine and Pope. Brogan promised around-the-clock surveillance and told us all not to worry. I figured we could count on serious protection for twenty-four hours and then we were on our own. It wasn't great, but at least it would buy us some time.

I'd already made up my mind that I was going to get the money to hire security for Catherine. I had a piece of property up north with a cabin on it that I used for cross-country skiing. It wasn't worth that much, but it was paid for and I could always negotiate a small mortgage on it. It would be enough to at least cover Catherine's guard full-time and spot the rest of us on a part-time basis. It was my last piece of money, but I had no complaints. The people had to come first. I figured Pope, Bridges, myself, and Clem Dunkin, who were all potential targets, would have to look after ourselves one way or another. I explained this all to Bridges and Dunkin, who both showed up at my hotel room about an hour after Hagen and Brogan had left. They both agreed to the plan, and Bridges thought it would be a good idea if we all let each other know where we were at all times.

After we'd concluded the business, Dani and I talked the others into going out to Golden's for dinner. Everyone was down and made some sort of excuse, but in the end, we roped them all in. We took our two boys in blue along and bought ourselves a dinner to remember for a long time. With the wine, the bill came to four hundred and twenty-eight dollars. No one had any cash, so I sprung on my credit card. I figured I still could get a little more stretch out of my plastic before it got recalled. It was worth the price. It cheered everyone up and gave us all the feeling that maybe we'd somehow pull it off despite the odds against us. The one thing every one of us at dinner had in common, excluding the two cops, was that we all wanted that movie to go.

The business at Ajax certainly hadn't scared me off. It had made me angry. I wasn't about to crawl under a rock and hide for the rest of my life. I figured I had a right to do what I was doing as long as it didn't hurt anyone or interfere with someone else's freedom. I was more determined than ever to see both projects through.

Despite my determination and outward exuberance, I was feeling low. I hadn't a clue where in hell I was going to find that money. Things were getting so tight I was beginning to wonder about day-to-day costs. I certainly didn't show it. I had to put up a good front for the others.

I figured I had them fooled. All, that is, except Dani. She didn't say much about it, but I knew she knew.

The next morning I finally made my appointment with my bank manager. He gave me the mortgage on the property, and I turned it over to the security agency. As I'd figured, the boys in blue disappeared early the next evening. Bridges and I had spent the better part of the day calling potential investors, but no one was interested.

Pope finally got through to the Right Honorable Minister for Economic Development, Malcolm Hennessey Devoir, but Devoir wouldn't see him for five days. That left us only another five before the option on the script ran out. Without some commitment from somebody, Kessler would walk and we'd loose the whole show.

Things were looking really grim. I began to realize just how grim when Bridges showed up later that night in my hotel room and pulled a gun out of his pocket.

He laid it on the coffee table.

"This one's yours," he said grimly.

Dani looked aghast. I picked up the piece. A .32 caliber six-shot Saturday night special. It was cheaply made. It was also loaded. I could see some corrosion forming around the ends of the shells when I flipped the cylinder aside.

"Where'd you get this?" I asked him.

"The Waterfront Bar."

I knew the place. I'd been in it a couple of times, looking up some tough characters I knew hung out there. It was near the docks, where the seamen from the lake ships hung out. It was a toss-up which was cheaper, the booze or the whores that hung out there.

"I got four," Bridges explained. "One for Pope, one for Dunkin, one for you, one for me."

"Have you given them out?"

"No, only to you," he said.

"Good, then forget it," I told him, taking the bullets out of the gun. "The last thing we need is the four of us running around like a bunch of cowboys shooting up the place."

"We need protection," he insisted.

"Not with these," I said, pulling him up short and showing him the cast lines in the metal. "At best, whoever pulls the trigger on this one has one chance in ten of blowing his own head off. The metal's as rotten as six-week-old hamburger."

He looked at me and pursed his lips. He nodded like he understood. "I'll dump them," he assured me, then left, taking the gun with him.

I wondered if he would.

Chapter Twenty

Dani was up extra early the next morning. I asked her why. She said if she got out early enough she'd be able to get some temp work.

I guess I must have looked surprised.

"We can use the money," she reminded me.

"Things aren't that bad." I tried to assure her as much as myself.

"Sure they are." She laughed, then added in a more serious vein, "I'm not afraid of a little work. Besides, it'll take my mind off things."

I knew she meant the guns. I had no real reason to try to stop her. She wouldn't be in any more danger on the street than she would be at the hotel or at Bridges's office. She was dead set on going anyway. So I kept my mouth shut and went off to Bridges's office alone.

Bridges was very subdued. He apologized for the night before and said he'd gotten rid of all the guns. He started to explain how, but I told him I didn't want to know.

We continued our calls and appointments. We both got turned down less and less, not because we were having any more success, but because there were fewer and fewer people to see. Pope called in and said he was at home watching television. Catherine was with Dunkin going over their lines at Dunkin's loft. The security guard had driven her over. Dani called and left her number when I was out for a few minutes. She'd gotten a typing job at the head office of the telephone company.

I took a spin out to Ajax in the middle of the afternoon when I ran out of people to call on the film deal. Jane Willson was in remarkably good spirits, considering what she'd been through. She'd already set the cleanup crews in motion and cleared a space for her drawing board in the old office. The construction crews were to be brought back after the cleanup. A number of the nonunion help came out anyway and insisted they wanted to work despite the fact that their salaries would have to be deferred until the insurance money came through.

Dani arrived back at the hotel about half an hour after I did. She was carrying a brown paper bag.

"I got an advance," she said, unpacking what looked like enough food to feed a small wedding party. "We're having deli for dinner. I hope you like chopped liver."

"Love it." I smiled. Actually I hated the stuff. But there was enough of an assortment to keep me from going without. Even if there hadn't been, it was the thought that counted. I told her about the chopped liver, just to set the record straight. I assured her it was the first and last time I'd ever lie to her.

She made me promise. We spent the whole night just being silly and really kind to each other.

The next morning we both got up feeling pretty damned good, certainly not like the world was against us.

"I got a feeling things are going to work out," she said, kissing me good-bye. She had another day at the telephone company.

I went off to Bridges's office feeling up. He was further down than I'd ever seen him. He wouldn't talk about it. He just kept repeating over and over that there wasn't anyone left to see.

I went back over my own record book. After going through it twice, I was beginning to wonder myself if he wasn't right.

The telephone rang at ten. It was our first call in or out all morning. It was for me.

The voice at the other end spoke good English with a hint of a foreign accent, probably mother tongue German or Swiss. He introduced himself as Mr. Kurt Schwarzer.

"I represent the Driscoll Corporation," he explained. "We're an offshore private investment banker. We've been looking at projects in Canada and your name came up. I've been told by a number of sources that you may have a project we might be interested in. Can we talk?"

"How about noon at Golden's," I suggested.

"I'm free this morning," he informed me crisply. "I understand you're in a hurry."

I wasn't about to get into an argument. Not with the first fish that had even given us so much as a nibble in weeks. I gave him our address.

"I'll be there in ten minutes," he said and hung up.

I told Bridges what had transpired. He had already guessed most of it. He started to gather the paper work to show the man. There was no way of trying to make the place more presentable. I'd managed to get it cleaned up a bit since I'd begun sharing it, but it was still your basic shambles. The hunt scenes were up on the walls, but the piles of boxes and film cans still took up half the floor space. There was no room to put them anywhere else.

Neither Bridges nor I had ever heard of the Driscoll Corporation, but then that didn't mean much if it was private. Besides we weren't exactly in the position of being choosers.

Mr. Schwarzer arrived on time. His voice certainly hadn't prepared me for his visual appearance. He was dressed in a six-hundred-dollar three-piece suit and was about normal in height. What seemed so incongruous was the head that poked out of the top of that suit. His features were thick and Negroid in character, but his skin was neither white nor black. Rather it was a mixture of both in broad, irregular patches, not a mulatto at all but more like a pinto. His head was as clean-shaven on top as a Brunswick bowling ball. A thin fringe of long, curly reddish brown beard ran along his jaw line from ear to ear. His eyes were half hidden by rimless glasses with photosensitive lenses. He carried a thin pigskin attaché case.

We introduced ourselves. Then I asked him how he'd heard about the project. I asked the question for two reasons. First, if I knew who turned him on to us, I might have an idea of what negative arguments might have already been raised. Second, if I knew who he'd been in contact with, I'd have a better chance of judging the league that the Driscoll Corporation was in. Similar-sized fish in the money game tended to swim together.

"Perhaps the question should be: who doesn't know about your project or your problems?" he said with a tiny smile.

He was right. There was hardly a person who dealt with money in the country who didn't know our situation. Just the same, he hadn't answered the question. I made a note of that.

"If you're worried about us," he went on, "let me assure you we don't waste people's time. We have more than enough to pick up National's share."

He'd done his homework and talked big enough. He was talking about a minimum of two million dollars.

"I'd like to see the books," he insisted.

We sat him down between us and went over the paper work. He knew his business and put us both through the wringer twice. When we were done, he asked a lot of questions about the talent.

He spent a lot of time going over head sheets of the actors and actresses. In the end, he seemed particularly interested in three girls that Bridges had marked as possible extras. One of them, Henrietta Burgundy, a tarty, full-figured twenty-two-year-old dyed blonde, was one of the bimbos Bridges had picked up around the studio and had been seeing off and on for the last couple of weeks.

Schwarzer handed the pictures back to Bridges and addressed us.

"My first impression is positive," he said. "Perhaps you two can join me for lunch. We'll talk more; then, if I'm satisfied, I'll speak to my people."

Bridges and I took him to Golden's. During the drinks, Bridges slipped off to use the men's room and, I found out later, to make a phone call.

Schwarzer was much more relaxed and personable during lunch. Both Bridges and I had the gut feeling he might go for the deal.

"You seem to know a lot about showbiz," Bridges said. "Has the Driscoll Corporation been involved before?"

"No, we're mostly in real estate and venture capital in electronics," he explained. "My personal background was show business. I'm the product of a Jewish German piano player and a black American jazz singer. As you can see, I'm equally uncomfortable with niggers, honkies, Christians, and Jews."

It was the kind of remark that only someone like Schwarzer could pull off and make funny. He said it without bitterness but with a kind of flavor that showed he had a good understanding of what he was and how other people saw him, at least on the surface.

"You don't mean Bettylou Mercer and Abel Schwarzer by any chance, do you?" Bridges asked with a look of surprise.

"The very same." Schwarzer smiled.

"I saw them in a cabaret act in Berlin. Must have been '37 or '38."

"Had to be '37," Schwarzer insisted. "They escaped to Switzerland at the end of the year."

Schwarzer went on to tell us how his parents established themselves in Geneva, where he was born two years later on the eve of Hitler's invasion of Poland. His parents had saved enough to send him to good schools, and after their deaths, the estate paid for his law degree at Harvard and postgradute studies at the London School of Economics. He had dual Swiss-American citizenship and spoke six languages fluently and another ten, including Chinese and Japanese, well enough to do business.

Henrietta Burgundy arrived halfway through the meal, seemingly by coincidence. I had no doubt Bridges had called her. Schwarzer turned his attentions to her but continued to charm us all. He'd been around the world a dozen times and his knowledge of almost any subject was encyclopedic.

The one thing he didn't appear interested in talking about was Driscoll. I tried once more to find out who had told him about the deal and who controlled Driscoll Corporation. Both questions were politely ignored.

"I'll promise you one thing," he assured me, "I'll have a quick answer for you, one way or the other. Perhaps even by Monday."

It was Friday. We were seeing the Minister of Economic Development on Tuesday. If anything came out of the Driscoll Corporation interest, it could dovetail nicely with our pitch to the government.

Bridges and I hadn't tried to hide anything from Schwarzer. He knew about our deadlines and the bind we were in. Even if the Driscoll Corporation came in for a hundred thousand to pick up Kessler's option it would help keep the shop open.

"My people will either play big or not at all," he insisted.

When we got ready to leave, Bridges offered Henrietta a ride home. She politely declined and went off with Schwarzer.

Bridges's only comment to me was: "I've been trying to get rid of that tart for weeks."

Chapter Twenty-One

Bridges and I checked out the Driscoll Corporation later that afternoon. We were able to turn up several apartment buildings in Metro that they owned but nothing else. Driscoll Corporation was a Liechtenstein resident, and there the trail stopped. I had little more luck checking out Schwarzer. I did find one lawyer friend of mine who had gone to Harvard about the same time. He remembered Schwarzer but could only say that he was an average student and an out-and-out loner. I checked with Harvard and found that Schwarzer belonged to none of the alumni or postgraduate associations. Nor did they have any further information on him except for a mailing address in Zurich care of the Haufstaeder Bank. The London School of Economics had even less.

Bridges and I decided not to tell anyone about Schwarzer. It was foolish to raise anyone's hopes on such thin prospects.

I did, however, tell Dani. I suggested we skip the leftover cold cuts and go out.

"It's not a sure thing. You said so yourself." She argued in favor of the cold cuts and eventually won.

We invited Catherine and Pope to come over, but only Pope showed up. Catherine was with Clem Dunkin. Again. We didn't ask for any explanations and Pope didn't offer any. He was extremely irritable, but nonetheless he finished the chopped liver before leaving.

Monday, true to his word, Schwarzer called and asked if he could see us. He arrived a few minutes later and removed two copies of a legal document, handed one to each of us, and instructed us to read them.

While Bridges and I read, he paced back and forth with his hands clasped behind his back.

The contracts had been drafted since we had last seen him. They included a number of very specific clauses relating to the documents we had shown him the day before. He hadn't taken anything away from the office, so I could only assume he had done the whole thing from memory.

The contract itself was a hard bargain. It gave Driscoll Corporation most of the profits and ownership control of the project. It still clearly spelled out Bridges's and my control on an operational basis. It did provide something besides money that we desperately needed—the completion clause which guaranteed the necessary money to finish the picture even if it ran over budget.

"We're being asked to give up a pretty large percentage of the total profits," Bridges argued.

"Yes, that's right," Schwarzer admitted, "but you're getting three million plus the completion guarantee."

"We still need another two million and a distributor. We may not have enough points left over to raise the rest."

"If you bring in the government, you won't have to worry about anyone else."

What he said made sense. The government would only want to be paid back for their initial investment. That meant Bridges, the Winnipeg dentists, and myself would still be able to share in the profits and recoup our investment. And we'd still have enough left over to hook a distributor on a percentage basis, using all his money for promotion. The only thing that bothered me was that we *had* to go with the government money if we were going to make the Driscoll deal work. The government money was far from a sure thing.

"We'd like a little time to think it over," I told Schwarzer.

He looked at me as if I was nuts, reached into his pocket, pulled out a check, and laid it on the table in front of us. It was a cashier's check made out to the production company for three million dollars.

He left it there just long enough for both of us to get a good look at it before returning it to his pocket. "I'll come back at noon," he said, then turned and left the office without even saying good-bye.

There wasn't much discussion. Both Bridges and I knew we had to sign. Neither one of us talked about it, but we both knew. If we didn't close some sort of deal quickly, we'd have to pull the plug on the whole business and write off all our time and everybody's money. Even with the little time we had left, there were few companies that would simply write you a check for three million without jerking you around for two or three months. But this was exactly what bothered me most. Who was the Driscoll Corporation? Where was the money really coming from? Did I really have to know?

Bridges and I went around and around. He wanted to sign. I wanted to know more. Our one out, he insisted, was the fact that we had to raise two million dollars elsewhere. If we were lucky enough to raise the whole five million elsewhere before the picture was shot *and* before the Driscoll Corporation money was drawn down, we'd be able to break the deal with the Driscoll Corporation. I didn't really believe there'd be a hope in hell of other money except maybe the government money, but at least we had an out. Even if we ended up not using the money, it would provide bait for other money.

Schwarzer returned at noon. I tried once again to find out about the Driscoll Corporation. This time, to my surprise, he opened up a bit.

Most of his clients are old European families who are looking for a safe haven for their money.

"Switzerland is only a few hundred miles from the Soviet border. The Europeans are very nervous these days."

"But why films? That's not exactly the safest place to put money," I countered.

"If you've done any checking at all, you'll find we have a number of real estate ventures and other investments. All of these are generating income. None of our investors want these revenues to go back to Europe. Most of the common market countries have currency restrictions, and there is a very good chance that any money that went back across the ocean would have to stay there. Of course, if the revenues stay here in this country, someone is going to have to pay taxes on it somewhere along the line. Your film project provides an excellent way of minimizing this problem."

"Then it isn't offshore money that's being invested," I said.

"The initial capital was offshore and I can assure you that if this formula works out to the advantage of my clients, this will be just the beginning of our investment in your film industry. It should work out nicely for everyone."

His story sounded logical enough. But there was no way to check it out without the names of his investors. I knew he'd never give me those, and I would have needed weeks, maybe months to track down the Driscoll Corporation owners, if I was able to at all. In the end, I had to accept what he said at face value if I wanted to play the game with his money.

Bridges and I both signed the documents, then went to my bank to deposit the check. It would be held in escrow until the other two million was in. The whole deal was wrapped up by one o'clock.

Schwarzer declined the invitation to lunch. He left us a number in town.

"I'll be traveling between here and the U.S. for the better part of the next six weeks. Then I'll be going back to Zurich. If you need me, call and leave a message," he instructed us cheerfully, then held out his hand. "Good luck."

We shook hands and Schwarzer was gone a moment later.

We set right to work drawing up a contract for the government. There was a good chance we'd get them in. We'd already brought in the first three million. There was a good chance, according to Schwarzer, that we might be able to attract more foreign money into the country. That would help our balance of payments' deficit as a country.

Bridges and I stayed up all night working on the

documents. Dani came by and brought us some Chinese food, then fell asleep in the padded chair in the corner. I woke her up about two in the morning and sent her home by cab.

By morning, we had the paper work finished. All it needed was a couple of signatures, and we'd be in business.

"They'll never sign this damned thing without a thousand changes," I said, trying to be realistic about the whole thing.

"Who knows, maybe we'll be lucky. Who'd have thought anyone would walk in the door and drop a check for three million dollars in less than two full working days," Bridges said in his best carnival voice. He slapped me on the back and said, "Think positive."

"Sure, why not." I grinned back with a positive smile that would have made Dale Carnegie proud. Maybe Bridges was right. Maybe our luck had really changed. It had, but not exactly in the direction I had hoped it would.

Chapter Twenty-Two

We met Pope at the airport and grabbed the eight o'clock to Ottawa. Our appointment was for nine thirty. We arrived in plenty of time, but Devoir kept us waiting. His offices were in the center block of the Parliament buildings on the fifth floor. There was a large reception area, two smaller private conference rooms which opened onto the reception area, a secretarial office behind the reception area, and finally, the Minister's office behind that.

Pope, Bridges, and I spent the first half hour going over our strategy, then spent the remainder of our wait in silence, reading the newspapers and magazines lying about. There wasn't much Bridges and I hadn't already gone through. We'd filled Pope in on the plane. There wasn't much he could do. Most of the presentation was financial. We needed him for moral support and because of his longtime relationship with Devoir.

Pope was in a strange mood. He was edgy and seemed preoccupied with something else. I figured it had something to do with Catherine and Clem Dunkin. I didn't think it was any of my business, so I didn't push it. On the other hand, I hoped he wouldn't let his mood get in the way of our pitch to Devoir. We needed all the help we could get. That *was* my business.

It was nearly noon when Devoir's secretary ushered us into the Minister's office. It was a spacious room, booklined, with a number of old framed photos of past prime ministers.

Devoir was, as usual, the embodiment of a tooth-paste commercial. He smelled faintly of aftershave lotion. His nails were perfectly manicured with a matt finish. His suit was the perfect banker's blue pinstripe. He wore a fresh carnation in his lapel.

He never seemed to stop smiling, although I got the feeling right from the outset that he didn't want to see us. He had a strong voice, which, despite the fact that he talked softly, had a way of penetrating through you. He would have made a good stand-in for God in DeMille's *Ten Commandments*.

We gathered around a large table opposite his desk. I noticed that both Devoir and Pope avoided any kind of eye contact with each other.

Devoir listened patiently as Bridges and I made our pitch. We showed him the agreement with the Driscoll Corporation and emphasized that if the venture was successful, it would likely attract additional offshore money. We also argued that the government had already signed a letter of intent.

"Yes, but that was conditional on National's participation," he explained.

"It's essentially the same deal," Bridges insisted.

"There are a number of trade-offs. The Driscoll Corporation isn't a picture distributor, but you've satisfied me that that can be managed," he said in his best conciliatory manner. These guys in politics had a special way of kicking you in the teeth and asking for your vote at the same time. I could see it coming.

"Unfortunately," he continued, "our problem now is one of timing."

"Mr. Minister, all we need is your signature. The rest of the paper work can be done afterwards," Bridges said.

Devoir shot Bridges a glance that could have cut diamonds. I expected a tongue lashing to follow. Instead, Devoir kept right on smiling and explained the situation to Bridges like he was dumb.

"A month ago, we had an entirely different situation, Mr. Bridges. Our financial resources, while far from unlimited, were available for projects such as yours. Today,

112

we're under a great deal of pressure to put these funds elsewhere."

"What he's trying to tell us is that the opposition leader, Pierre Lemoux, has the Minister's nuts in the wringer and won't let go," I explained to Bridges, who, being British, hadn't yet picked up all the finer points of native politics.

The Minister winced visibly at my remark but responded positively, figuring I was an ally or at the very least I understood the problem. I understood his problem all right, but I wasn't in his bed.

I knew the government was in a tight spot and was trying to buy off Quebec with more money for make-work projects in that province. I couldn't argue that the plan might not be politically desirable and buy votes in the short run. On the other hand, it wouldn't bring any money back into the country. While the movie business was at best a risky venture, it did have some chance of paying for itself and fueling the economy.

"I understand your argument, Mr. Nevers, but I still have Pierre Lemoux to deal with," Devoir insisted. "Maybe in a month or two things will be different. We should definitely keep talking."

He stood up to signal the meeting was over. "I have a cabinet meeting at one," he said, gathering up a folder of papers on his desk. There was little we could do to argue the point. Bridges and I headed for the door. Pope walked up to the Minister and said a few words that neither Bridges nor I could hear. We only heard Devoir's response. A low hiss which said: "Absolutely not."

Pope turned on his heels and joined us as we left the offices. His eyes were narrowed and his mouth drawn tight. He wouldn't look at either Bridges or myself on the elevator ride down. He walked well ahead of us as we headed toward the main doors of the building.

On the way out, Bridges asked me who Lemoux was. By chance, we passed him in the hallway coming from the Parliament chambers. As usual he was surrounded by a group of media types and was giving his usual impromptu news conference.

"The guy in the wheelchair," I said to Bridges, pointing Lemoux out in the crowd.

When we were out of earshot, I filled Bridges in. Lemoux was a one-time labor leader who had a tremendous grass-roots following in French Quebec. He had been a leading organizer of the Quebec separatist movement and was probably its second most popular political proponent after René Levesque, who became the first separatist Premier of the province in 1976. Lemoux had been Levesque's right-hand man and together they had managed to gain complete control over language, education, culture, telecommunications, broadcasting, transportation, most areas of law, and a number of other key areas, which in effect had already given the province a defacto separation from the rest of Canada. So much so, in fact, that the strategy of the separatist party had changed completely.

Once, the provincial separatists had shunned federal politics to show their contempt for the nation as a whole and to emphasize their status as a separate nation. The separatists now actively participated in federal politics. There was no fundamental change of heart. The separatists were still dedicated to breaking up the country. Their sole reason for participating was to drain as much federal money back into the province as possible before the political division actually and irrevocably occurred.

"The nationalists don't want us to separate," Lemoux was fond of saying, "so maybe by the time we're done picking the chicken clean, they'll kick us out."

The federal government was slowly losing control over the province, despite the fact that it was dumping billions into Quebec to try to stem the tide of separation. In Quebec, Lemoux was regarded as a hero. He not only was a champion of the French separatist cause but also was responsible for bringing home a larger and larger piece of the bacon. No one in the province, which boasted the highest tax structure in the whole of North America, was ungrateful for that.

Lemoux had won a special place in the heart of his supporters and enemies alike when he had become the victim of an assassin's bullet. Nearly two years before, he had been attending a hockey game with René Levesque at the Montreal forum when a gunman had attempted to shoot the Premier in front of the refreshment stand during the break between the second and third period. Lemoux had thrown himself between the assailant and the Premier and had grappled with the assailant. Only a single shot was fired. It pierced Lemoux's stomach and shattered his spinal column on the way out. The gunman escaped in the confusion.

Lemoux wasn't expected to live the night. However, the feisty member of Parliament not only lived but was well enough to resume his official duties within six months, despite the fact that he was permanently paralyzed from the waist down. There were many in Quebec and elsewhere who believed the assassination could have been part of a grand conspiracy aimed at destroying the separatists. The official word from the Royal Canadian Mounted Police and the Quebec Provincial Police was that it was the work of a lone person. No evidence had ever been uncovered to contradict or affirm this point of view.

Chapter Twenty-Three

We caught up to Pope in front of the U.S. Embassy. He was holding a taxi for us. We got inside and drove out to the airport. Despite our initial depression, there was still some hope. We had a check for three million dollars in the bank and a "maybe" from the Minister of Economic Development. On the negative side we had an option that ran out in four days. Without the script we had no movie.

By the time we reached the airport, Pope had opened up.

"You didn't handle him right at all," Pope told us both in no uncertain terms.

"You just sat there like a bloody ass," Bridges shouted at him.

The taxi driver pulled over to the curb and told them both to stop screaming or we'd be walking.

Pope looked like he was going to have a go at the taxi driver. I grabbed his arm, turned to the driver, and said: "Drive."

The driver turned back and started to drive.

"What the hell am I supposed to know about money?" Pope asked Bridges in a subdued but angry tone.

"You didn't have much trouble convincing him the first time," Bridges reminded him.

"He wanted to be convinced that time."

"You better convince him again, damnit. Because you're finished if you don't. No one's going to take another chance on a drunk, coked-out Hungarian director with a track record like yours. You're finished," Bridges told him.

It was hitting below the belt, but I could see what Bridges was doing.

"Jesus, you think I want to see this picture go down the tubes?" Pope squirmed.

Bridges only stared at him and shook his head. "You poor sonofabitch," was all he said.

We rode the rest of the way to the airport in silence. Pope kept running his thumb and forefinger together across the underside of his lower lip.

Bridges and I got out of the taxi first. Pope got out and told the driver to wait. Then he asked Bridges for four copies of the contract we'd drafted for Devoir.

"Maybe if I talk to him again, I can get something moving," Pope said as he climbed back into the cab and headed toward Ottawa. Bridges and I watched the cab as it drove away.

"You think one of us should stay?" I asked Bridges.

"No, whatever it is he's got to do, he's got to do it alone," Bridges replied.

We caught the two forty-five back to Toronto.

I dropped Bridges off downtown and drove out to Ajax to check things out. The cleanup crews were about halfway through. Jane Willson was as chirpy as a bird and had done a whole new set of drawings.

"I think I can improve the watering system," she told me, showing me the preliminary rough sketches. "There may be some good coming out of this after all."

She walked me around the plant and pointed out where she thought she could improve on her original design and save on lighting costs as well. I left later that afternoon to meet Dani for dinner. She had invited Catherine and Clem Dunkin along. We all had a pleasant dinner at Golden's, with the possible exception of the maître d'. Dunkin did one of his special pratfalls and looked as if he had broken his left leg. I'm sure that was the first time the maître d' ever got a twenty-dollar bill for showing four people to their table and not calling an ambulance.

As much as I wanted to hate Dunkin, I couldn't

help liking him. He was tiring and hyperkinetic, but there was something infectious about his perkiness. He made Catherine laugh almost continuously with his fly in his soup routine, his fly in his cordon bleu routine, and his fly in his salad routine. I could see it was just what she needed to bring her out of her depression. They had a funny sort of relationship, more brother and sister than lovers. Certainly that was the way they projected it around Dani and myself. Clem Dunkin was Catherine's greatest fan and never tired of singing her praise. Catherine nagged like a mother hen at Dunkin to be good, to not do this or that.

We all took in a double feature at the Roxy where one of Catherine's old movies was playing. We dropped Dunkin and Catherine off separately. Catherine was staying at Pope's apartment. The security guard was inside the lobby waiting for her and he escorted her upstairs.

Dani and I went back to the hotel. When we reached my room the phone was ringing. I opened the door and walked across the room in the semidarkness to pick up the receiver. Even in the light from the hallway, I could tell something was wrong. Dani came in a pace behind me and flicked on the light just as I picked up the phone.

I looked around at the room. It was all my furniture, but everything had been completely rearranged. The bed was in the sitting area. The desk had been moved to a different wall. Even the two Tabriz carpets had been switched between the two rooms. I held the receiver to my ear.

"It's Clem. Am I bothering you?" Dunkin asked.

"Just a minute," I told him and covered the speaker with my hand. I looked at Dani, who was looking around the room quizzically. "You didn't decide to redecorate, did you?" I asked her.

"Me? Whatever for?" she said in a voice with just the slightest hint of nervousness. She walked slowly about the room while I continued on the phone to Dunkin.

"Sorry for the interruption. What's up?"

"Someone's broken into my place. They didn't take anything. They just rearranged the furniture."

"Any idea who?"

"No, but they left this crazy note. I don't know if it's for real or some kind of joke," Dunkin explained.

"What does it say?"

At the same time Dunkin was reading the note, Dani found a similar one propped against the lamp on my desk. She brought it to me. It was the identical note that Dunkin read to me over the phone. It said: "God has the memory of infinity. He shall not forgive if you continue with the movie. You have been warned." Both were signed with an octagon with a cross inside and two crossed shepherd's staffs behind the octagon.

"Enough people owe me for all the stunts I've pulled, but what do you make of it, Billy? Is it for real or a gag?" Dunkin wanted to know.

"It's for real, Clem," I told him.

"The funny thing about it is that I checked all the doors and windows," he went on. "They're all locked shut from the inside."

Chapter Twenty-Four

I had Dani call Catherine and make some girl talk. I wanted to find out if anything had happened at Pope's place, without coming right out and asking her, in case nothing had. Certainly, if the furniture had been rearranged, she would have noticed. Nothing unusual had taken place, so I assumed the guard had been a sufficient deterrent. I called Bridges at his hotel room. He was asleep. Yes, his furniture had been moved, but he thought it had been the management. He looked around and found an identical note from the Flock of God people. I told him to come right over.

Dunkin arrived shortly after Dani got off the phone with Catherine. Bridges came in fifteen minutes later. We had a long talk and all came to the same conclusion— that we'd have to risk the publicity and call the police.

I tried to talk Lieutenant Hagen into coming down and handling the case himself. Again, he had to turn it over to the beefy Lieutenant Brogan, who was handling the Flock of God file. Brogan told us he'd keep it out of the newspapers, then promptly set an army of detectives loose combing the Ritz and Bridges's hotel and the streets near Dunkin's loft, looking for anyone who might have seen something or someone strange in any of the areas. They turned up nothing. No one had seen or heard anything.

Miraculously, despite all the inquiries, no one in the media picked up on the story. I was glad for two reasons, Catherine and Jane Willson. I drove out to Ajax early the next morning. It was business as usual for Jane and the cleanup crew. Since Catherine hadn't been bothered, I figured we'd made it through this one with a minimum of damage. I was a bit concerned about Dani because of her association with all of the target people, especially me. I'd talked this over with her on several occasions. She insisted there was nothing any of us could do.

"Besides that," she reminded me, "the Flock has never physically hurt anyone in all their acts of violence."

I wanted to believe that, but then again, there could always be a first time. I wanted to put a special guard on Dani, but she talked me out of it, saying that she'd try to lose the sonofabitch the first chance she got.

"The only kind of men I like following me around are the ones that I'm going to end up in bed with. The rest of them can go to hell," she joked, pulling me into bed and insisting that we were both tired from all we'd been through that day. For a girl, she had some pretty smart ideas.

The latest Flock of God incident had one good effect. It took our minds off the fact that there were only three days left to come up with the option money for Kessler. Both Bridges and I tried to reach Pope in Ottawa, but he had disappeared again. I doubted very much that anything had happened to him. He called Catherine several times but refused to return our calls.

To make matters worse, several other pictures had started production in the last two weeks. A lot of the best crews were already hired out for the next eight to ten weeks. We had lost the best cameraman in the country for eight weeks. Bridges was still confident that there was enough talent left in the city to do a good job.

The difference between the best and the second best," he quipped, "is the best will always save you money by doing it right the first time."

The way things were going it was beginning to look like there wouldn't be a first time. The money people were all hiding or not answering their telephones. The government bureaucrats were giving us "maybes." The studio wanted to know whether or not we were going to pay for another week. Our money ran out there the same time that Kessler's option came due. If we didn't give the go-ahead, they'd strike the sets that we'd already begun to build. They were being nice about it since no one else wanted the space. But time was running out and business was, after all, business, the manager of the studio reminded me. On top of that I had a pack of loonies running around loose somewhere trying to stop the film. The police had been totally unable to get a line on any of them. It was like they never existed or came out of some hole in the ground to do their dirty work, then disappeared back again when it was done.

Finally, there was Kessler. I hadn't heard from him in nearly two weeks. But I hadn't stopped thinking about him. There was something eerie that made him as potentially dangerous as the Flock of God cult. I remembered the weird effect he'd had on Dani the night he'd come over to argue his point about the film. I thought once or twice about asking her about that but decided in the end not to dig up old graves.

I did ask Bridges about Kessler during one dull afternoon.

"He'll come around for the money," Bridges assured me. "For all his big talk about the integrity of the script, his bottom line is money. If it wasn't, he'd still be making two-fifty on the *News* instead of trying to win an Oscar the first time around."

Bridges wasn't much help, so I let the whole thing drop. I had no doubt that if the question was never answered and I made it to old age, it would be one of those curiosities I'd be able to chew over as I reminisced about my filmmaking days. For all intents and purposes they were part of my past. Despite the Driscoll Corporation money, neither Bridges nor I had been able to raise the slightest interest among the moneylenders.

My filmmaking days might have slid neatly into the bad memory slot and passed from view in another two days if Pope hadn't suddenly appeared late that afternoon at Bridges's office. In more ways than one, I wish he hadn't shown up like he did. It's strange to think how such a little twist can change so much. And not all the time for the better. But then, you sometimes don't know that until a long, long time afterwards, long after it's too late to do anything about it.

Pope had the surliest of grins on his face. He walked up to each of us and handed us a copy of the contract we had prepared for the Minister of Economic Development. My copy was signed in the clearly legible handwriting of Malcolm Hennessey Devoir. I could see from the expression on Bridges's face his copy was signed too.

"I'll be a sonofabitch," Bridges said, grinning from ear to ear.

"Next time maybe I don't bother with any producers. I just do it myself," Pope snarled.

Bridges ignored his remark and just kept repeating: "You did it, you sonofabitch, you did it."

"I showed him, didn't I," Pope said to me.

"I guess you showed us all." I clapped him on his back before he got a chance to clap me. I did it just hard enough so he'd think twice before returning the gesture.

"Hey, take it easy," he said, coughing and trying to catch his breath. "We still got to make the picture. And you need one smart director to make it into a hit."

There wasn't a lot of time for celebration. Pope took off immediately to the studio in Kleinberg to get things going out there. He intended to start shooting in two days and wanted to have everyone on the set the next day for a walk-through.

Bridges and I headed right to the bank. We didn't have a check from the government, but we had the next best thing. The bank manager said it would take another day or two to clear through the paper work, but he assured us we could start drawing down the money the next day. Once this had been arranged, Bridges took off to Kleinberg to help Pope. I was given the task of locating Kessler. I'd already written him a check for a hundred thousand to pick up the option. Bridges had made it easy for us to deliver the money. He had opened a production account for Kessler and had been paying him through that. Regardless of whether or not I found him in person, all I had to do to fulfill our side of the obligation was deposit the money in this account. As it turned out, that's what I had to do. I tried every contact that Bridges and Pope could think of, but no one had seen him in weeks. The list that Bridges and Pope had given me wasn't long. Kessler was an out-and-out loner. When I called the *News,* where he used to work, I couldn't find a single person who would admit to being his friend.

After depositing Kessler's check the next morning, I went out to Kleinberg to see how things were going. Dani had gone out at six. She'd gotten her call from Pope the night before. She was busy working on alternative designs for one of the sets and didn't even have time to have coffee with me. But she was happy and that was all I really cared about.

The studio where Pope and Bridges had set up shop was a hive of activity. Bridges was busy signing checks. There were a good number of overdue accounts and money that had to go into escrow for salaries for the crew. There was a renewal on the studio facilities, which gave us a full eight weeks on the set and an option for another one-to-four if we needed it. I co-signed about seven hundred thousand of the five million dollars that first day. Counting Kessler's option, we'd almost reached the million mark.

Pope was as busy as Bridges. Outside he was directing a double crew of carpenters who were throwing up the first finished sets and doing the finishing work on the interiors. Pope walked me through one of the sets and pointed proudly to the work.

"This morning we had a hole in the wall. Now we have a boudoir that would have made Jean Harlow green with envy," he said, showing me around the bedroom.

I was amazed at how fast it had been thrown together. It was the hotel room where Catherine St. Catherine's character carries on her torrid love affair with Clem Dunkin's character. Everything was in place, down to the French ivory comb and brush set on the vanity. But it wasn't just a replication of a bedroom. Each wall could be swung completely free of the room. The furniture was built onto special tracks so it could be moved back and forth to accommodate the film and sound equipment and the dozen or more people who would be behind the camera during the shooting.

"I start with the love scenes." Pope grinned at me. "Catherine begs me not to start with the love scenes. She says: 'They're the hardest. Give us time to warm up to them.' It's precisely because they're the hardest that I want to start with them. Do you understand?"

"Maybe she's right," I said. I only offered the comment because he asked. I'd never been a part of this kind of thing before. What did I know about creative types. The last thing I wanted to do was pick a fight with Pope or tell him how to run his business.

"No, she's not right, and I'll tell you why," he said, walking me next door to a second set where the carpenters were putting the finishing touches on an authentic-looking Irish pub. It would be the main meeting place for the IRA and where the plan would be hatched between the Nazis and their Irish contacts. "Actors and actresses, if you give them the chance, will take a year to get ready for a part. They are never ready. You must always drop them head first right in the water. The good ones swim. The bad ones"—he shrugged—"let them find another profession."

It struck me as ironic that Pope was now into the bully role. If Bridges hadn't browbeaten him on the way to the Ottawa airport after we had the meeting with Devoir, Pope might not have talked Devoir into signing. Now it was someone else's turn to play the shit kicker, and someone else's, again, to play the shit kickee.

Chapter Twenty-Five

On several occasions I asked Pope point blank how he'd managed to talk Devoir into signing the contract.

"Continental charm." He laughed.

I never did get a straight answer out of him. Not that it really mattered. The money was in. That's all that counted. The picture was definitely in production.

After the first day of shooting I'd been invited to view the rushes. Pope was there with his assistant director and his cameraman. Catherine and Clem Dunkin were noticeably absent. Dani had come as my guest.

Ten seconds into the footage, I had to ask myself whether or not the whole film venture hadn't been the biggest mistake in my life. I was watching close-ups of Dunkin and Catherine in bed. Over and over again, I saw takes of the same scene. Catherine fellating Dunkin, even after he had lost his erection. All the while I could hear Pope chuckling to himself.

Pope turned around from his front-row seat and looked over at me. I could see him leering in the half-light from the projector.

"She threw up after that take," he said, indicating the sequence we had just seen. "But she got it right the next time."

Dani and I stood up at exactly the same time. The reason we'd stayed even that long was because of the pure shock of the pictures. The whole thing had an unhealthy stench to it.

If Pope noticed we had gone, he made no attempt

to say good-bye. Neither Dani nor I spoke on the long drive back to the city. It was the first night since we'd been together that we didn't make love. We both fell asleep just hugging.

The next day I called Bridges and told him about the rushes. I said we'd have to control Pope or he was going to blow the whole thing.

"I take it you only stayed for the first few minutes," Bridges said.

"About three at the most," I replied.

"It's not as bad as you think. I saw the rushes earlier. If you'd stuck it out for ten, you'd have seen them with their clothes on," Bridges informed me. "I'd say, not a bad piece of work for the first day."

"But what a way to get it," I remarked.

"It's his way. He'll probably shoot five minutes of sex with those two every time they're supposed to say hello. It's his way of getting them to put out their utmost. I don't exactly approve, but on the other hand, it works."

I couldn't tell one way or the other. I had to accept Bridges's word for it. I knew one thing; if that was what making movies was all about, I didn't want any part of it. I'd seen slaughterhouses that were more humane.

I wasn't about to get uptight about the production. Bridges assured me all the hot scenes would end up in the garbage anyway. On the other hand, I decided to keep my distance. There weren't a lot of reasons for me to hang around the studio anyway. All I was doing was providing the second signature on the checks. Bridges came into the downtown office late each afternoon, so we set up the session there.

Dani worked out at the studios every day, but she wasn't directly involved in the filming each day. She saw Catherine from time to time . Dani thought she was holding up quite well. She'd begun to lean even more heavily on Clem Dunkin for support.

The gossip mill had Catherine and Clem as a hot item, but Dani was more skeptical.

"It won't last," she insisted. "Catherine's stuck on Pope. In the end she'll go back, although God only knows why. I don't know what she sees in the man."

That one short conversation was about the only time in nearly a week that we had discussed the movie, outside Dani's specific job. She did tell me about the designs she was working on.

Kessler finally showed up, or rather, called. He went on for a good fifteen minutes about how Pope and the rest of us were going to destroy the film and make it into a pile of garbage. He said he was still going to do everything in his power to stop the film, but his voice sounded defeated. I didn't think he believed it himself. Still, he reminded me that if principal photography was not complete within three months, he still retained the right to buy the property at our cost plus ten percent. Even if the film stopped shooting that day, that would have amounted to more than two million dollars. Nevertheless, it was conceivable that he could buy his rights back if we fell on our faces.

For my part, I spent most of my time out at Ajax. Jane had started the construction of the interiors again, and I handled the paper work in the office to give her more time with the construction crew.

I was perfectly content to take a back seat in the movie business, and I probably would have if I hadn't gotten a frantic call from the bank manager on the tenth day of the shoot.

He wouldn't explain over the phone. I asked him if he'd talked to Bridges.

"I've already called him. I think you'd both better be here for what I've got to say."

Chapter Twenty-Six

I was in the bank manager's office in thirty-five minutes. Bridges hadn't shown up yet.

"Suppose you tell me what's on your mind," I said.

"As soon as Mr. Bridges arrives." He spoke nervously, "I want you both to hear."

There wasn't much I could do but wait. Whatever it was, the manager thought it was important enough to have all his calls held while he stared at me across the desk or pretended to be reading some papers.

There weren't any magazines around, so I entertained myself by taking in the sights. The brass desk set had an inscription which read: "To Edwin D. Harway, for twenty-five years of dedicated service." He had a picture of a middle-aged woman, kind of chunky and, I presumed, his wife, in a gold frame on the bureau behind him. Beside it stood a second picture in a matching gold frame with two teenaged boys who looked like a fair compromise between Harway and his wife. On the wall were a number of framed documents certifying that Harway had passed through the system and was acceptable to meet with the public and handle their money.

Harway himself was tall, once probably athletic but now sporting a noticeable pot. He was bald on top. His suit was an expensive doubleknit about four years old. He was trying to be calm, but I could see he was a wreck. Twice he lit a cigarette, took one puff, and butted the whole thing out. Once he lit the filter end and apologized for the smell.

After waiting forty-five minutes, I called the studio. Bridges had left over an hour and a half before and said he wouldn't be back. That was more than enough time to reach the bank. I called his downtown office and the hotel, but no one had seen or heard from him all day.

There was nothing we could do but wait. It was about five o'clock. The tellers had closed their stations and were cashing out. I was getting tired of waiting.

"Maybe it's better if I get hold of Bridges and we come back first thing in the morning," I suggested, getting to my feet.

"No." His voice cracked. "Please sit down. We have to take care of this immediately."

"I don't see how we're going to do that. Maybe Bridges got stuck in traffic. Maybe something else held him up. Whatever it is, by this time he probably figures you've closed up and he won't show up anyway."

"Damn," was all he managed.

"If you need both of us, we'll be back in the morning," I said, heading for the door.

"No, wait," he practically yelled. His secretary poked her head through the door.

"I'm leaving," she said, looking me over suspiciously, "if you don't need me anymore tonight."

"That's fine, Mrs. Grason. I won't be needing you anymore this evening. Thank you." He smiled at her coolly.

"I've left word at the front door to let Mr. Bridges in," she told him.

"Thank you. See you in the morning."

She closed the door again but not before she gave me the dirtiest look. I half expected her to push the silent alarm to see if I was in on some robbery or extortion scam.

When the door was closed, Harway invited me to sit down again.

"You should both be here," he said, shaking his head and taking a file from inside his desk. It was a thin file. I could see right off it contained copies of the contracts we had signed with the bank, the Driscoll Corporation, and the government.

He removed the government contract from the file and opened it to Devoir's signature.

"We have reason to believe this document has been improperly executed," he spoke crisply.

"If it's some technical point . . ." I said before I was interrupted.

"According to the Minister's office, this document is no good."

"But the Minister signed it," I said, hoping against hope we were talking about some slight legal technicality and not, as the pit of my stomach told me, about some very large and serious problem.

"According to his office, the Minister signed no such document." He expelled a long sigh. I quickly realized Harway was an unwilling ally. He wanted to believe I was telling the truth. He wanted to believe the whole thing was a very bad joke.

"I'm sure it's just a misunderstanding." I tried to smile. Maybe Devoir had signed it and forgot to tell the proper subordinate. There were certainly enough pigheaded bureaucrats in the nation's capital who'd tie up a napkin if it came across their desk.

"And maybe it's a forgery," Harway blurted out, then followed with another "Damn." He shook his head sadly. "Do you realize what this could do to my career? I'll be lucky if they give me Labrador on my next posting."

Harway, when all was said and done, was a gentleman. He could have had me arrested on the spot. On the other hand, the original contract with the Driscoll Corporation exonerated the bank from any liability if fraud was perpetrated by either the production company or Driscoll. In effect, all the money that had been spent to date had been the Driscoll Corporation money. If anyone was going to put me in jail, it was going to be them.

"I've checked with our head office," Harway informed me. "They instructed me to clear this up as soon as possible. I, of course, had to Telex the Driscoll Corporation in Zurich to contact me as soon as possible, but so far they've not responded."

From the way Harway laid it out, he didn't know about Schwarzer's in-town telephone number. I wasn't about to tell him. Zurich was probably asleep when the message came in. So, with any luck, I had a few hours' grace before the shit hit the fan.

I assured Harway I'd clear up the whole thing by morning and headed for the door.

"Whatever you do, please keep it out of the papers," he pleaded.

"I'll try," I told him. That's the one thing that banking people all have in common. A paranoia about the press. Any inference of hanky panky with the bank's money, no matter who's at fault, is always bad publicity for the bank. I knew I could count on Harway not to go spreading the bad word. That assured me I'd picked up the benefit of the time difference between Metro and Zurich.

I went back to the hotel feeling like I'd been hit by a truck. There was a message from Dani that she'd be late. I was glad I wouldn't have to drag her into the problem and sorry at the same time because she wasn't there to talk to. She'd become a real friend in a short time. That's more than most people get from their lovers in a lifetime. She was the one person I figured I could say anything to and get an honest opinion back. She was the only one who'd shared her cold cuts with me in a long time.

I tried to reach Bridges and left messages everywhere I could think of for him to call me immediately. I tried Pope too, but he'd left the studio and hadn't arrived home. Catherine hadn't seen him since late afternoon and was having dinner with Dunkin. I also left word for Pope to call me. I was even more interested to see him than Bridges. Pope had been the one who'd brought the signed document back from Ottawa. It ran through my mind to call Devoir directly, but in the end, I decided that was a bad idea for two reasons. If he had signed it, there was no sense getting him involved in trying to straighten things out at this point. If he hadn't signed it, then I didn't think I'd want to run around publicizing the fact that I'd been using a forged document to raise money. There was always the possibility that he had signed it and now was denying it. A long shot, but nevertheless a real possibility.

I'd been waiting an hour when the phone rang. I picked it up, expecting Pope or Bridges. Whoever it was was talking so low I couldn't understand them.

"What?" I barked into the receiver, thinking maybe it was a badly connected long distance call. My first guess was Schwarzer.

It wasn't. The voice repeated itself, this time loud enough for me to make out what was being said.

"Stop the movie or you'll die," it said. I couldn't tell if it was male or female, but I had no doubt about the source. The Flock of God people had come back to haunt me at a really bad time. Under normal circumstances, I might have thought twice about what I did next. But these weren't normal circumstances and I wasn't thinking.

"Listen, and listen good, shithead," I yelled into the receiver, "get off this fucking phone. I'm expecting a very important call."

I slammed the receiver down hard enough to break eardrums. I stood there and stared at the phone for two long minutes, just hoping they'd call back so I'd get another chance to tear another strip off them.

Sure enough the phone rang again.

"You're one dead sucker if you don't get off this phone and stay off." I spoke in a cool, deadly voice, all business and no nonsense. I really didn't have any idea what I was going to do next if they didn't get off the phone or kept calling back. I had no intention of carrying on a dialogue though and was in the process of slamming the phone down again when I heard: "Billy, is that you?"

This time I recognized the voice.

"Bridges?"

"Yes, what was that all about?" he asked.

"You didn't just call, did you? No, never mind," I said, answering my own question. "Where are you?"

"I'm back at my hotel. I just got your message."

"Do you know where Pope is?" I asked.

"Not a clue."

"See if you can find him," I instructed him. "But whatever you do, don't leave the hotel room. I'm coming right over to talk."

"All right," he said. His voice sounded very tired.

The way he sounded confirmed my worst fears. It had been a sigh of resignation. Bridges had gotten the same call from Harway that I had. I'd showed up because I didn't know what was going on. He probably *didn't* show because *he knew*. But just what he knew and how bad the bad news was, I still had to shake out of him. It was going to be one unpleasant evening.

I called Dani at the studio. She was just leaving. Catherine had gotten the same threatening call I had. Hers had been left with her answering service. She'd gone back to Clem Dunkin's loft with the guard.

"I suggest you go there, and wait for me. I've got to go out on some business. I'll come by and pick you up when I'm on my way home," I told Dani.

"For God's sake, Billy, nothing's going to happen to me. I've had a long day. I'd just as soon go to the hotel and take a nice hot bath."

I tried to talk her out of it, but she insisted on coming back to my place.

"If you don't think bad thoughts, nothing bad will happen to you," she said cheerily.

Since I couldn't come up with any good thoughts, I asked the hotel security to keep an eye on my place.

Chapter Twenty-Seven

The door to Bridges's room was slightly ajar. I knocked. When no one answered, I let myself in. Bridges was sitting in an easy chair by the bed in the dark. I turned on the light.

From the smell and the half-empty bottle, I could tell he'd recently worked himself through twenty ounces of sherry. He jumped up a few moments after the lights were on like someone had stuck him with a cattle prod. His eyes blinked like a night toad caught in a set of oncoming headlights.

"How are you, Billy?" he said, more tired than sodden. He stuck his hands in his pockets as he spoke. I had the feeling it was a defensive move meant to show me he was unarmed, in case I was going to take a poke at him.

"The government contracts are forgeries, aren't they." I came right to the point.

"Yes." He nodded.

"Were you in on it from the beginning?"

"No, I only found out about it three days ago. One of Devoir's people, one of the bureaucrats I'd been dickering with before our trip to Ottawa, called and said he might be able to find some money in the department if we wanted to resubmit our proposal on a smaller scale. I didn't know for sure until I made some other inquiries with people who should have known if Devoir had signed anything. It wasn't hard to put two and two together when no one knew anything about our contract."

"Why didn't you tell me right away?" I asked.

"What was I going to tell you? That we'd both end up in jail? Half the Driscoll Corporation money was already gone. I've spent the last two days padding everything I could find to pad. That's why I didn't show up at the bank this afternoon. I was busy siphoning off every penny I could before they locked up the account. What the hell else could I do?"

"I don't know," I told him. Bridges had acted like anyone at the helm of a ship about ready to sink. He'd tried to buy time. Only in this case it was a little like throwing the women and children overboard to make the boat float better.

"You figure Pope forged the signatures?" I asked.

"It had to be him. I don't know anybody else crazy enough."

"Did you find him?"

"No. He was at the studio when I got the call. I think he knew what was up. For all I know, he might be into one of his disappearing routines."

"We'll have to find him sooner or later to get a handle on the details. We're still flying blind."

"What do you think we should do in the meantime?" Bridges asked.

"There's nothing we can do, except wait for Zurich to phone. The bank isn't going to touch us. They're afraid of the bad publicity. It all depends on the Driscoll Corporation. It's their move."

"Then you think we should continue with the production? I'm sure I could keep us going for ten days, maybe two weeks."

"Let's see how Schwarzer reacts. We could all be eating lunch in jail by tomorrow."

Bridges nodded solemnly.

"We'll meet at the studio at nine. If Pope's going to turn up anywhere, he'll turn up there. In the meantime, if you hear from him, tell him to call me at the hotel," I said.

I turned and left. I was halfway back to my place when I realized I hadn't asked Bridges if he'd gotten a threatening call from the Flock of God people. Somehow it didn't seem that important.

Dani arrived back at the hotel a half hour before I did. She'd had her bath and was stretched out on the couch like a cat in her satin kimono. She was reading a great big fat novel.

"I'm just at the most exciting part." She smiled and looked up at me for a second, then dove back into the last few pages.

It gave me enough time to change and pour myself a drink.

"You want one?" I asked.

"Scotch," she said.

I poured a second one. When I brought them over, she was just finishing the last page. She closed the book and laid it on the coffee table, then patted the sofa for me to join her. I sat down beside her. She rested her long legs across my lap and sipped her drink with her back resting against the arm of the sofa.

I looked at the book she'd been reading. It was Martin Renzlag's latest mystery *"From a Dead Man's Point of View,* ten months on the *New York Times* best-seller list, as the cover said.

"I didn't know you were into mystery books," I said.

"I'm not. They scare me too much. But one of the girls in the studio gave it to me at lunch and said I just had to read it."

"You read all that since lunchtime?" I was really impressed.

"No." She laughed. "Just the last chapter. I always read mysteries backwards. Less scary that way. Besides, then I get to see how the author wrote it."

That's what I liked most about Dani. She always had a fresh way of looking at things.

"I'm sorry I was such a bitch on the phone," she apologized. "Now that I've had my bath, I feel just wonderful. Here, smell."

She held out her arm.

"Smells like dessert," I said.

"Wild Blossom," she informed me. "How was your day?"

If she was dumb, I might have gotten away with a simple "Wonderful, honey" parted her kimono, and buried

137

my troubles. Maybe I should have tried that route, but I didn't.

"Not good," she said with a sympathetic little pout.

"Not good," I agreed.

I told her the whole story about the bank manager, what Bridges had said, and what we expected Pope had done.

"The bottom line is that we've spent about a million and a half of the Driscoll Corporation money illegally. God knows how they're going to take it. I know if I was in their position, I wouldn't be very happy. I guess the worst that could happen would be that I'd go to jail and everyone would have a dandy tax write-off from a straight loss." I laughed.

Dani didn't laugh. She stiffened noticeably. She lifted her legs off my lap and put her feet on the floor. She was sitting with her back straight, the same way I was sitting but at the other end of the couch.

She looked at me, then turned away and stared straight ahead. All the color had gone out of her face. Her fingers played nervously with the hem of her kimono, which she'd pulled tightly around her as if she was cold.

"I knew I'd have to tell you this sooner or later," she said. "I hoped and prayed that I wouldn't have to, but I knew I would."

"Tell me what?" I asked gently. The only other time I'd seen her act like this was the night Kessler showed up at the hotel.

I started to move toward her, but I saw her visibly stiffen, so I backed off.

"I'm a prostitute, Billy. A hooker. I had five arrests for soliciting by the time I was twenty-two."

"That's a long time ago, Dani. Whatever happened then . . ."

"Was and am," she said, cutting me off. "I met Catherine four years ago in Los Angeles on a double date. She knew what I was. It didn't bother her. I was luckier than most. I didn't have a pimp and I didn't belong to anybody, so I got to make my own decisions. I knew I'd already peaked in the business, and I had to start looking around for something else to do in my old age.

"Catherine took me on as a project. Maybe she does have more of her father's blood in her than she'd like to admit. Anyway, Hollywood people are always looking for causes. Jerry Lewis has muscular dystrophy. Catherine has me.

"She found me jobs around the studios. When things got bad for her in California, she brought me back here. She's been good to me, and as far as she's concerned, I'm one hell of a reformed whore. For the most part she was right. But sometimes, when she wasn't paying attention, I'd step out. Nothing regular, just when it was convenient and I needed a little extra money for this or that. Mostly friends of friends. That sort of thing."

"Pope?" I asked.

"Yes. The first time I met you I was doing him a favor. Catherine didn't know a thing about it. For all her foul talk, she's a lady underneath. She'd have died if she'd known."

"Outside Bridges's office?"

"Yes, some accident. I was waiting in a coffee shop around the corner. Bridges called as soon as you left."

"Bridges, too?"

"Yes. They were both in on it. I wasn't supposed to be running off to meet anybody. I was supposed to end up going home with you. When I saw you again, I just couldn't go through with it. I'm not some kid who believes in love at first sight anymore. I don't know what I believe in, and I don't know what it was. I guess I just liked you. That's all. I told myself that somehow maybe it could be different with you. I don't know why. I just had a feeling, and for once in my life I wanted it to be that way."

"After that?"

"I told Pope and Bridges to forget it. Pope wanted me to be with Farrell King. I only went to dinner that night because I knew you'd be there. I don't expect you to believe me, but I *wanted you*. Being with you made me feel better than I had a right to feel, but damnit, I wanted to hold on to that.

139

"When Kessler showed up that night at the hotel, I freaked out. He knows about my past. It was suddenly like I was a whore in a hotel room again and it shook me. I couldn't do that to you, Billy.

"The next day I realized how silly I was being, and I tried to make up to you. So I made love to you like some whore. I woke up and you were still asleep. I was so mixed up, I just ran. I don't really know why. Maybe because I felt that you'd somehow know about my past from the way I loved you. Maybe because it felt so funny to enjoy it with you. I don't know why. It doesn't really matter.

"What mattered was that I knew I couldn't run very far. I knew I'd have to see you again. I knew I'd do anything to keep on seeing you. You know, Billy, when I went out those two mornings to work for the telephone company I really did work for the telephone company typing up letters. I loved every minute of it because I realized I was going home to you.

"I just wanted you to know all this before you get that call from Zurich tomorrow," she finished off and took a deep breath.

"What's this have to do with Zurich?" I asked.

"Everything." Her face was like stone. "I'm the one who turned the Driscoll Corporation on to you."

I just looked at her, trying to take all this in.

"It's mob money, Billy," she blurted out. "If anything happens to their money, they'll kill us both."

Chapter Twenty-Eight

It wasn't a laughing matter. I'd in effect just taken about a million and a half of the mob's money and flushed it down the toilet.

The Driscoll Corporation, Dani explained, was a European laundry operation for the powerful Mosconi family of Montreal and, more recently, of Toronto. The Mosconis had the unique distinction among criminal families of being the subject of simultaneous inquiries by the Senate in the U.S. and by a Royal Commission in Canada.

The Mosconi empire stretched over most of Quebec and had strong ties in the New England and Mid-Atlantic States. The recent inquiries into organized crime had shown the Mosconi family to have extensive connections in meat packing, transportation, gambling, drug distribution, prostitution, loan sharking, and coin vending machine leasing and sales. More than thirty gangland and bad debt slayings in the past four years were linked indirectly to them. Despite the extensive investigations on both sides of the border, no criminal charges had ever been made.

The patriarch, Guiseppe Mosconi, made his home in Montreal. His three sons, Ronald, Alfred, and Benjy, lived in various suburbs of Toronto. I knew all this from reading the papers.

What I didn't know was that Dani at one time had traveled in the same circles as the young Mosconis and had a passing acquaintance with the old man. It was

141

Ronald Mosconi, the eldest and heir apparent, whom she finally called in the darkest days of our fund-raising efforts.

"You were so desperate, Billy. I just had to try something. I figured if you believed in it that much, you could make it work," she explained.

If Pope hadn't double-crossed us, it would have worked out okay. There wouldn't have been any way anyone could have gotten hurt. Now I at least understood why Schwarzer had been so eager to write the deal so we'd *have* to go after the government money. Any government involvement would make their investment legitimate beyond a reasonable doubt.

"Does Bridges or Pope know about the connection between the Driscoll Corporation and the Mosconis?"

"No, at least not through me." She shook her head. "I shouldn't have done it. I was stupid, but I guess there're certain things that are just too late to change."

She turned and faced me. "I'm sorry, Billy. I really am."

She started to get up. I grabbed her wrist and pulled her back down. She turned and stared dully at me without emotion.

"Where do you think you're going?" I asked.

"I told you everything I know, I swear." She spoke with a slight tremble in her voice. "I just want to go now if you're finished with me."

She started to get up again. I pulled her down roughly. When she tried to pull away, I squeezed her arm hard enough to let her know I could hurt her if I wanted to.

"I'm not through with you," I said. "I want you to listen and listen good. What you've done before you met me doesn't matter a damn. What you did with the Driscoll Corporation was stupid maybe, but only because it worked out in a way that certainly wasn't your fault. As far as you and I are concerned, I'm not much of a romantic either, but I know what you and I've had has been damned good for me because it's made me feel good."

I stared hard at her and saw I was getting through. She wasn't trying to pull away. I relaxed my grip on her arm.

"Dani, they say that two people in a relationship don't really know each other until they've had their first fight. So we'll count this as our first. They don't say you ever have to have a second one. Maybe we'll be that lucky. Now, you're free to go if you want. I'm not going to hold you here. But before you go, I want you to understand that I want you to stay."

She just looked at me and her big brown eyes filled with tears. She cupped her hands over her face and began to weep.

I took her in my arms and held her to me. She was crying so hard she was gasping for air like she was drowning. I held her for an hour until she stopped trembling. I thought a lot about what she had told me. Maybe it should have bothered me, but it didn't. I felt good that it didn't.

Dani was on an early call, so she left before I got out of bed. I pulled myself together at eight and fought the traffic out to Kleinberg. The traffic was the least of my problems.

When I arrived at the turnoff to the studio grounds, I found the entrance blocked by half a dozen sign-carrying pickets. The signs read: "Boycott *CRASH*," "No Scabs," and "Support 801w."

I edged the car to a stop with my bumper lined up with the kneecaps of the most forward of the pickets. They were a burly lot. It looked like reruns of Saturday afternoon wrestling.

One of the pickets came to the passenger side of the car, opened the door, and got in.

He was maybe thirty-five, going on forty-five, with a face that looked like a scrubbed potato. His eyes had about as much sensitivity as the headlights on a subway train.

"You're Billy Nevers, aren't you," he said. "We had our boys do a make on your car."

"Am I supposed to be impressed?" I asked.

"The name's O'Shea, Donald O'Shea," he informed me. He didn't offer his hand and I didn't offer mine. "I'm the head of Local 801w. You know about us no doubt." He narrowed his eyes at me.

143

I knew what 801w was. The national trucking union had absorbed a number of smaller unions a few years back. One that had been absorbed was the Motion Picture and Television Workers Union, the "w" in 801, and the same 801w that all the technicians on the shoot belonged to, or so I thought.

"You got me at a bad time, Mr. O'Shea. So give it to me fast and straight and we'll both get on with our business."

He eyed me like a dog eyes a fire hydrant.

"You and I are gonna have to face off across that table soon enough. If we can't do it there, then we'll have to do it somewhere else," he spat. "But one thing I want to get clear right from the beginning. I'm not dumb, so don't bullshit me."

"If there's a problem, I'm sure we can work it out," I said, trying my best conciliatory tone.

"Work what out?" He exploded. "You got a full-scale production going with a nonunion crew."

"You're kidding," I said. It was all I could think of saying. I'd had so many surprises I couldn't come up with anything else. My response was so totally dumb that it even caught O'Shea off guard.

His eyebrows nearly touched as he eyed me carefully.

"Do I look like someone who kids?" he asked.

O'Shea looked like the kind of guy that hadn't smiled in five years. I'd been watching the other pickets out of the corner of my eye. They'd moved off the road and were standing beside a small fire to keep warm. I knew that I wasn't going to clean up the problems with O'Shea to anyone's satisfaction. I figured once he got out of the car, his boys would try to block my way in. I'd told Bridges I'd meet him at nine. It was three minutes to. I intended to keep that date.

I did the only thing I could. I hit the gas and took off like a bat out of hell down the studio road before anyone had a chance to react.

The road was posted at fifteen miles per hour. I was doing seventy-five. O'Shea didn't move a muscle. Every drop of blood was gone from his face.

144

The parking lot was full. I hit the brakes and fished into a space in front of the door to the main building. I turned to O'Shea.

"You can wait here or you can come inside and we'll give you a cup of coffee to warm you up. I'll be more than happy to speak to you when my meeting's over. In either case, if you wait, I'll drive you back to your buddies. But right now, I got other business to take care of."

He looked at me with his face in a rage. When he talked, he flicked his tongue in and out like some bug-eating creature.

"You just signed your own death warrant," he snapped as he let himself out of the car. He slammed the door and started the hike back to the main entrance. I wasn't about to run after him.

I flipped the keys to the security guard and told him to let me know if any of the goons came around.

Chapter Twenty-Nine

Once inside the building I realized the union goon squad had already been at work. There were a couple of black eyes and some bruises but no major damage. I'd been in too much of a hurry when I came through the parking lot to notice that a few of the cars had had their lights bashed with rocks.

Catherine was tending to the wounded like Florence Nightingale and acting as general morale booster to the others in the cast who were waiting to start the day's shooting. One makeup girl was trying to cover a bruise on Clem Dunkin's upper lip. When he saw me, he smiled. "Maybe we should shoot the bar-room brawl scene today."

I nodded and went looking for Dani. She was at work at her drawing board.

"You okay?" I asked her.

She just smiled and gave me the thumbs-up sign and went back to work. The rest of the crew was out back setting up.

I found Bridges and Pope in the back office. Neither would look at me when I came through the door.

I sat down and pointed to Pope.

"Okay, you're first," I said.

"Hey, señor, first about what?" He sniffed in a bad imitation of a Mexican accent.

"When did you forge the contracts?" I asked patiently.

He looked from me to Bridges and back again at me like I'd just arrived from the moon.

"What? Forgeries? Like I told Bridges, I don't know what you guys are talking about. Really, man." He sniffed again and gave me a big coke grin.

He'd grown up in Hollywood where everyone has a little scam of some sort on the side. As far as he was concerned, this was just another of the same.

"Now, you can play funny if you want, Pope," I said. "But whether you know it or not, you're a walking dead man."

He just grinned until I started to explain the Driscoll Corporation connection, the fact that the Mosconis were involved, and more than a million and a half of their money was gone.

"Me and Bridges, we'll probably just get a neat bullet in the back of the head. When they find out you were the one who set them up," I explained, "they'll probably skin you alive by drilling a hole in your belly and sucking out your guts with a straw."

It was the nicest way I could think of putting it. Pope's grin sagged and he looked sick to his stomach. He could only manage to talk in a whisper.

"I swear, Billy. Devoir gave me his word he'd sign, then he started to stall. I know he'll come through," Pope explained.

"I just hope you're right," I said, dismissing him for the time being and turning to Bridges. "Now, what's all this union problem?"

"I had to do it, Billy. The other productions in town had thinned the ranks of the best technical people more than I had first imagined. We need good people. We can't afford second-rate. There's enough first-class people in this town who aren't in the union to do five pictures. If it's any consolation to you, we're paying union scale."

I nodded and filed the information away for later in the discussion.

"We've got one more problem. Several of the key people on the film, including Catherine, Dunkin, and myself, got threatening calls, presumably from the Flock of God people."

"I got one last night too," Bridges informed me. "Right after you left."

"We got a number of good reasons for closing down production. One, no money. Two, the possibility of violence from the Flock of God people. Three, possible violence from 801w. At the same time, we got a number of reasons to keep going as long as we can. Basically, it's our only hope of getting the government money to finish the picture and our only hope of coming out even with the Mosconis. The Mosconis are good enough reason by themselves for trying to finish the film. But let's not kid ourselves, chances of that are a hundred to one or worse.

"We got a lot more to consider than our own asses," I insisted. "If we pull the plug now, only the two of you, myself, and Dani have to face the Mosconis. If we continue, we got a lot of innocent people out there who could get hurt. They've got to have a say."

"They want to do this picture," Bridges assured me.

"That's right." Pope backed him up.

"Maybe so, but we're going to ask them and they're going to get a chance to choose. It's their show as much as ours."

Both Bridges and Pope reluctantly agreed.

We held a meeting with everyone present. I didn't go into the details of the Mosconi money because that only concerned Bridges, Pope, Dani, and myself, but I made it clear that there was a very good chance we would have to close down the production for financial reasons in the near future. With that as the bottom line, I talked about the possibility of violence from the Flock of God people and the union group.

"Our stand is to keep the production going as long as possible and hopefully get this movie made," I concluded. "I can't and I won't ask any of you to stay. But I will keep your jobs going as long as possible."

The room buzzed with whispers when I finished. Catherine got up right after me and declared that despite the dangers to herself, she felt it was her duty as an

148

artist to see the production through. She got a standing ovation.

She was followed by a gaffer by the name of Patrick Terry. Terry was a bit of a roustabout and had caused a couple of hours' delay one morning while he threw a fit over the lighting of one scene. Pope had told me about it, because the cameraman had almost walked out when Pope refused to fire Terry. Pope resolved the feud by shooting the scene both ways. It turned out in the night rushes that Terry was right.

"I'm not good at speaking," Terry began, "but I know my lighting. Before anything happens, I'd just like to thank Mr. Bridges and Mr. Pope for taking a chance on me. Now, I'm not pretending to speak for anybody else. Just for myself. And I'm not against the union. They do a pretty fair job for the fellows that belong. The trouble is, they want me on a three-year waiting list before I get a chance to work. I'm willing and able to work now. If there's work, I think we got a right to choose whether or not we take the job. I'm for staying."

He sat down and there was more whispering among the group.

"We're not going to take a vote," I said. "This isn't a group decision. It's got to be an individual decision. If we have enough of you to go on with the production, we'll carry on. That's that. Anyone who wants to leave, we'll draw your check now for your full pay through the rest of today. Anyone who wants to stay, I suggest you get back to work. You've got a tough schedule ahead of you."

"Let's get on with it," Terry said, and the meeting broke up.

Only three people came forward during the day to collect their pay and check out—one technical person and two extras. Ideally I would have liked to send Pope back to Ottawa to talk to Devoir, but we had to be satisfied with the telephone. I needed him on the set to keep the production going and keep morale up.

By the end of the day, Pope had located Devoir, and Devoir promised to talk to him later that evening. Pope assured us Devoir would sign in the end. Pope seemed so sure that even I started to believe him, although I knew how crazy that was.

Neither Bridges nor I called Harway, the bank manager, mainly because there was nothing to tell him. When we left the studio that evening we left in a caravan of strength. The union goons were gone. I had a good idea they'd be back, but I figured we'd have to deal with that when the time came. We had set up a buddy system among the talent and crew so that everyone would be able to keep a check on everyone else. If there was trouble of any kind, they were to call either Bridges or myself.

Despite the obstacles, we were somehow still afloat. The most curious thing of all was that more than twenty-four hours had passed since Harway had sent the telegram to Zurich. We hadn't heard a peep out of Schwarzer. I kept praying that maybe we wouldn't. But I knew that was too much to ask.

Chapter Thirty

Harold D. Kessler called late that night. He'd heard about the union goons on the set. He also had heard rumors about financial trouble.

"I'm glad," he told me. "But I don't think you know why."

Frankly, at two in the morning, I didn't care. But just to get him off the phone I promised to meet with him the following morning at Bridges's downtown office.

He seemed as jittery as usual. He certainly hadn't spent any of the hundred thousand on clothes. He looked like he'd just crawled out of a garbage can behind the Salvation Army.

He didn't have much new to say. Mostly it was the same old story about how Pope was going to ruin the story and ruin his one big chance.

"You understand money, Mr. Nevers. When I first signed the deal with Pope, I didn't have the best advice. I signed away all my rights. That means Pope can have someone else do the book and anything else that comes out of this."

"Listen, Kessler, for an unpublished author without any track record in films you picked up a hundred and twenty thousand dollars and you still have four points on the film. So if the production company sells the book, you share in those profits."

"I'll end up with sixty thousand after taxes," he whined.

"I sympathize but what can I do. If you want a good tax shelter, invest in the movies."

"Very funny." He eyed me coldly.

"Look, my advice to you is to sit down and do another book. If you spent half the energy writing that you did whining, you'd be able to come up with another book or movie."

He stood up abruptly.

"You still don't understand," he said. "That's the only one I got."

He left in a huff, slamming the door on the way out. I thought I understood what he meant at the time. But I hadn't, and I didn't find out until much later.

I arrived out at the studio at eleven. The union people were still nowhere in sight. The production was rolling along and had actually picked up the lost time from the day before. I left for Ajax in the middle of the afternoon to check on things there.

Work out there also was moving along ahead of schedule. Part of the insurance money had come through, and Jane had paid up the back salaries of nonunion employees and recalled the unionized workers.

I drove back and had a quiet dinner with Dani. Two days had passed, and there was still no word from Schwarzer.

Pope continued to assure me that he was making progress with Devoir. There was no way for me to check, short of calling Devoir myself. I didn't think I had a chance of getting through to him. Even if I did, I'd probably only have put a crimp in Pope's negotiations, if, in fact, he was getting anywhere. We were all living day-to-day. While on the surface things were going well, I had a singular feeling of bad being right around the corner.

On the other hand, everywhere I turned, things *were* getting better. Bridges was stretching every dollar farther than we could have hoped. The Flock of God people and 801w had not come back to bother anyone. I was beginning to believe we might make it, in spite of myself.

I got a call on the weekend that I hadn't expected.

I recognized the voice right away but couldn't place it until the speaker identified himself.

"This is Malcolm Devoir, Mr. Nevers." The Minister of Economic Development spoke. "Mr. Pope has asked me to call you to tell you personally that, yes, the government is reconsidering your film proposal and I might add, appears to be favorably disposed."

"Mr. Minister, that's the best news I've had in a long time," I told him.

"I must caution you," he continued, "these things do take time, as you can well appreciate."

"You know our bind," I said.

"Yes, Mr. Pope has made me well aware of that. I'm sure we'll be able to work something out."

He said he would be in touch as soon as his government was in a position to move, then hung up. I wasn't sure if I'd just been handed a bucket of crap or a deal, but I was happy that Pope had at least gotten through. There was indeed hope. I phoned Pope and he just snarled.

"I told you so, didn't I?" he said and hung up the phone. I told Dani, and she said Pope was in a bad mood over Catherine. She was coming home to Pope every night, but about two in the morning. He was starting to give Clem Dunkin a hard time on the set.

I called Bridges and told him about the call from Devoir and asked him about Pope and Clem Dunkin. Bridges told me not to worry for the time being. It was still under control. Pope was making Dunkin go over and over scenes even when he'd done them perfectly. The more he got on Dunkin's case, the more Catherine took to defending Dunkin. This only made Pope madder.

"Typical Hollywood." Bridges dismissed it. He assured me that it had a lot further to go to reach the breaking point. He was much more excited about the call from Devoir. He figured we just might squeeze another ten days out of the money that was left.

"We'll leave all the expensive shots for last," he said. "We just might make it if the government can get off its damned ass."

I got off the phone. Dani and I went out and had a

153

very nice celebration dinner. As it turned out, it was premature.

The next day all hell broke loose. The union sent a caravan of twenty-five goons up to Kleinberg. I had gone out early in the morning to Ajax but came right over as soon as Bridges called. When I got there, the battle was over and the goons had left, but they'd taken a toll. The ambulances had taken three of our people off to the hospital. One was Patrick Terry. No one was sure how many from the union had been injured. They'd removed their own and driven away in their own cars after an hour of fighting. Clem Dunkin estimated probably five or more of their guys would need some sort of medical attention. The others backed up his figures.

I checked with the hospital. Terry had a broken leg and several broken ribs. One of his assistants, Lenny Edwards, was in serious condition with a fractured skull and unidentified internal injuries. The third person injured was a script girl by the name of Kate McCarthy. She'd taken a punch in the jaw and had a hairline fracture. There were a lot more superficial but rather painful injuries at the studio.

I wasn't there more than ten minutes when I got a call from Donald O'Shea, the union head.

"That's just a sample of what you can expect," he told me.

"You can expect ten years in jail," I informed him.

"Don't be stupid, Nevers. I wouldn't use my own people. You'll never pin anything on me or 801w. We're clean."

I hung up, knowing that the police would be called and they'd turn up nothing, just like O'Shea said. If the police were extra diligent, they might eventually pin something on the potato-faced cretin, but that might take years. For the immediate present, we were essentially on our own.

As executive producer of the film, I called everyone together and said under the circumstances we couldn't risk continuing. I'd just have to shut down the production.

I got exactly the kind of reaction I had hoped for but hadn't really expected.

"No, never, we'll fight," they yelled at me, shouting me down. The attack on Kleinberg had made them angry, not scared. When we did take a vote, it was unanimous, down to the last man and woman, that we try to carry on. I mean unanimous because I voted to fight, too.

There was no way it was going to be easy. We had to hire extra guards, which would cut seriously into the number of days we could continue shooting. We were also down by three good people, but there were enough left to carry on.

I started getting a little weird about Dani working out there. Despite the fact that I was ready to lay myself on the line, I couldn't help feeling protective toward her.

"I don't want you feeling like you have to stay out here because you feel you owe me," I told her in one of my less bright moves.

She put me straight in a hurry.

"I may owe you a lot, Billy, but I owe myself this one. There's a lot of decent people out here taking a hell of a lot of flak. And the only thing they've done wrong is take work that was offered to them. I can get behind it for them and for me. It all comes down to the freedom of being able to give someone a chance. It's my chance as much as theirs," she explained.

She came with me after work to visit the hospital. Kate McCarthy had been released. Her father had called the studio early in the afternoon and said she wouldn't be in for a few days. Several of the people in the studio had tried to reach her, but her father wouldn't let her take any calls.

Lenny Edwards had gone from serious to critical and was in Intensive Care. He had lapsed twice into a coma.

The only one that we got to see was Patrick Terry. His leg was in traction. He grinned when he saw me coming through the door.

"Hey, I heard you tried to pull the plug," he said.

155

"I just gave everybody the choice," I explained.

"If you'd managed it, I'd have personally strung you up by the balls." He laughed, then said to Dani, "No offense, Miss Davis."

"If he had closed us down, you'd have had to fight for the privilege." She laughed and sat down beside the bed, pulled out a pony of Irish whiskey, and poured us all a round.

The head nurse came in and told us we were making too much noise. When she saw the liquor she started to get uppity and insisted it wasn't allowed.

Ten minutes later, Patrick Terry, the fellow who couldn't talk very well, had her downing her own drink and promising to come back and visit the rascal later that night.

Chapter Thirty-One

The next morning, the studio looked like a circus. Local 801w had more than thirty pickets out marching with placards saying "Stop *Crash,* "End Scab Labor Forever," and other such things. It was an orderly demonstration and was made up mostly of legitimate members of the union. They were joined by several dozen university students, who were carrying their own signs promoting Marx, Lenin, and Mao slogans.

Interestingly there were an equal number of other students who had come by, although they were less vocal and less organized. The second group picketed the pickets because they supported our right to work.

The pickets for Local 801w made no attempt to stop anyone going in or out of the studio. Partially this was because we had hired fourteen armed security guards and had posted them at strategic positions around the studio area. Partially, it was because the union had put itself on its best behavior now that the media was handling the story.

In fact, the only real trouble any of our people had was getting a parking space with all the media vehicles that had descended on the area to cover the story. Even the U.S. networks had sent up crews from Buffalo.

The battle at Kleinberg had already become a minor *cause célébre*. O'Shea had gone on national television the night of the incident and publicly decried the violence. He went so far as to suggest that we may have staged the whole thing ourselves to get publicity.

He conveniently forgot about Lenny Edwards, Patrick Terry, and all the others who had real bruises to show for his handiwork.

Under normal circumstances, the story should have died, but it was one of those slow news times and the national news media milked it for all it was worth. In two days, it became the focal point for a national debate on the merits of collectivism vs. the freedom to work. Editorials were written supporting one or the other side. Newspapers across the country were deluged with letters to the editor decrying and applauding both sides. Several people even sent us dollar bills to help support the cause. I turned the money over to the United Way, but I filed it in the back of my mind that if things got really rough maybe we'd try to raise money to finish the film by turning it into a charity.

Somehow, despite the turmoil, Bridges and Pope kept production rolling. But Bridges warned me, and I could see from the books, that the extra guards were straining our finances. He estimated we only had six days to go before the doors were closed. I leaned on Pope to step up his negotiations with the government.

Somehow I had allowed myself to get deluded into the prospect of the government coming through in the end. The whole relationship between Devoir and Pope was strange to begin with. What was even stranger was that, in the end, Devoir called me instead of Pope. I was at my hotel. This time I recognized the voice.

"Mr. Nevers, this is Malcolm Devoir speaking," he said in a decidedly less friendly tone than he had used the last time.

"How can I help you, Mr. Minister?" I asked.

"As you know, we have been examining your film project in great depth for a number of weeks. I might add that we were rather favorably disposed. However, the events of the last few days have seriously altered our view. As you can imagine, any involvement in your project at this time could be seen as taking sides. For this and a number of other reasons that I'm not at liberty to discuss, I must inform you that the government cannot participate in your project. I'm truly very sorry, but I'm sure you understand."

"Now, wait, Mr. Minister," I slammed into him. "You can't string us along for all these weeks and then bail out. You made a promise. Isn't your word worth anything?"

"Mr. Nevers, I'm a very busy man. I don't have time to explain the facts of life to you. Your movie is politically unfeasible for my government to participate in at this time."

"There won't be another time."

"I'm sorry, then." He hung up. I stood there listening to the dial tone for ten seconds before I put the phone down.

I called Pope at home. I told him about the call from Devoir and what he said.

"That motherfucking cocksucker," Pope bellowed. "That's not what he told me."

"Listen, if he told you something else, then get hold of him and straighten it out. Just between you and me, we're living on borrowed time. We haven't heard anything from our friends at the Driscoll Corporation but you can be sure they haven't forgotten about us. Bridges says we can hold on for maybe three to four days more."

"I know all that, damnit. He promised. Devoir gave me his word," Pope insisted.

"If you can reach him tonight, call me back. If not, we'll have to have a session tomorrow and map out a couple of contingency plans. There's not a hope in hell of getting that money anywhere else."

I got off the phone and filled Dani in on the parts of the two conversations she hadn't overheard. She took it calmly. We both did. The emotional system can take just so many ups and downs before it begins to tune out. I told Bridges the bad news, and he had reached the same point, a kind of numb resignation.

The next morning, Dani had an early call and left before I got up. I was on my way to the car in the underground parking lot when I heard footsteps behind me. I turned and saw two men coming slowly toward me.

159

They were looking right at me. They were well dressed but that didn't hide the fact that they were big and solid-looking. I was only a few yards from my car. I opened the door and got inside.

Donald O'Shea was sitting on the passenger side.

"You're not going to win," he informed me.

"What are you going to do, O'Shea, have me murdered?"

"Maybe it could come to that. I think you'll come around. I hear you're smart and you like money."

I looked in the rear-view mirror and saw the other two hanging around the back of the car, waiting for a signal from O'Shea.

"Are you offering me a bribe?" I asked.

"If you get an offer, and remember I said 'if,' count yourself a very lucky man. My associates don't like to give away hard-earned money. There's a lot better ways of getting cooperation."

"For instance."

"Let me put it to you this way. It would cost someone a lot less to fill you full of lead, dump you in the trunk of a car, and leave you in the airport parking lot than it would to pay you off. So think about that."

It must have been my lucky day. The hotel security was just changing shifts. The two day-men had just pulled into the lot and were nosing their car into an empty space. I hit the horn, and they were both out of their car in a second. This was one time I was glad I hadn't forgotten them at Christmas.

Jack Cardley, the older of the two, came straight to the car while Tom Arkland, his partner, stood in the middle of the garage keeping an eye on the two over-dressed pals O'Shea had brought along.

"Everything all right, Mr. Nevers?" Cardley asked me.

"Just a little horn trouble, Jack," I assured him. "These fellows were wondering about monthly parking rates. Perhaps you could escort them back to the booth."

"We'll talk again," O'Shea said as he got out of the car. He walked quickly away with his two friends.

160

"You sure everything's all right, Mr. Nevers?" Cardley asked again.

"Just fine, Jack. But you keep an eye out for those three. If you see them around the hotel again, you let me know."

"Sure thing." He tipped his hat and I drove off.

On the way out, I realized that there was half a chance they'd come after me again. I didn't expect they'd come back with a payoff in cash either. The union was rumored to have a very close affiliation with organized crime through the Truckers national. With the kind of media coverage the event had gotten, it could very well be worth somebody's trouble to blow me away as an example. It was, however, an academic question because there was every reason to believe that we'd be closed down by the end of the week, union or no union.

When I arrived at Kleinberg for my meeting with Bridges and Pope, I was starting to believe it might even be sooner.

Pope had disappeared again.

Chapter Thirty-Two

Pope hadn't shown up and no one knew where he was. Catherine said he'd left in a taxi before seven that morning, but he hadn't told her where he was going or when to expect him back.

On top of that, a number of the cast and crew had received mimeographed cards through the mail which read: "Stop the movie or die." It was signed with the familiar Flock of God coat of arms.

A few of the more defiant members of our group had punched holes in the corners of the cards and had suspended them on strings around their necks or made them into armbands.

Patrick Terry, who came by that morning in his cast, suggested the slogan might be a good title for a best-selling book. He was a little put out he hadn't received a threatening card in the mail, so he borrowed one from the assistant cameraman and plastered it on his cast.

In a funny way, I was glad the cards had shown up. It took everyone's mind off the fact that Pope wasn't there and that production had ground to a halt. On the other hand, there was still a real danger that the Flock of God people would show up and try to deliver on their message. The fact that O'Shea had visited me that morning wasn't lost on me either. Those cards could have been sent by Local 801w, for all anyone knew. Or for that matter by anyone else who had a grudge against the film, including Kessler.

In the end, those of us who hadn't received them hadn't been overlooked. For some reason, the post office took as long as five days to deliver some, but when the final count was in, everyone, including Patrick Terry, Dani, Catherine, Pope, Bridges, Clem Dunkin, myself and all those who had been missed on the first day, received the identical cards. By that time an awful lot of dirty water had passed through the pipes.

As it turned out, Pope hadn't disappeared at all. He had flown to Ottawa on the first plane out that morning. He called us at Kleinberg just before ten and instructed Bridges and me to get the next plane out and meet him in Devoir's office as soon as possible. I pressed him for details, but he wouldn't give me any over the phone.

Bridges and I were in Devoir's office at quarter past noon. Devoir looked angry even when he smiled and shook our hands. Pope looked like he'd had a hard night.

"I called you here to witness the Minister's signature on our original contract," Pope informed Bridges and me. "Just so this time there's no mistake."

Bridges and I both looked at Devoir. He looked back at us and nodded reluctantly.

"Mr. Pope is a very convincing fellow," Devoir remarked. "You should be proud you're associated with such a man." There was an edge of sarcasm in his voice, but he was serious about signing. He pushed his intercom and his executive assistant, a thin, almost prim man, came into the room and stood beside the desk, waiting for his instructions.

"I'll need you to witness some signatures, Preston," Devoir told his assistant. The man nodded.

Pope picked up the Minister's pen off his desk and handed it to Devoir. Devoir shot Pope a veiled angry look as he took the pen and signed his name. We all witnessed the signature.

Devoir dismissed his assistant and the man left without ever speaking a word.

Devoir looked at the three of us and smiled. "That's it, gentlemen. Now, if you'll excuse me, I'll get on with the business of state."

There was no shaking hands, no thank-yous and no good-byes. The three of us, Pope, Bridges and myself, let ourselves out. Pope carried several copies of the contract and had given us one each to hold. On the ground floor of the Parliament building, a young man about twenty-five approached us. He addressed Pope.

"You kept me waiting an hour. What's up?"

Pope introduced us all around. The man's name was Roger Wiliker. He was a reporter for Canadian Press.

Wiliker wasn't in the mood for socializing.

"Look, you said you'd have something for me. Now if you don't have anything, just say so and I'll go get lunch."

Pope handed Wiliker a copy of the contract.

"If you can read, you got a good story for yourself," Pope sneered at the reporter.

Wiliker flipped through the contract. It was apparent from the first paragraph that the government had committed itself to supporting the film. Wiliker didn't need to be backgrounded. The story had been floating around for days, and it was the general opinion of everyone that the government would never come in on the deal.

Pope had already walked Bridges and me away from the reporter. Wiliker came running after us as we hurried toward the street.

"Hey," he called, waving the contract, "does this mean the government supports the right to work?"

Pope spun on his heels just as we hailed a taxi.

"No comment," Pope shouted back at the reporter.

A few moments later, we were in the cab and heading back toward the airport.

Bridges and I both pumped Pope on how he got the Minister to change his mind, but he wouldn't tell us anything. He sat grimly silent all the way back to Metro.

The news broke on the wire service before we even landed. Devoir went on television that night to defend his stand and to convince the nation that he had supported the project on the basis of its potential to bring badly needed foreign revenues into the country and not because the government was anti-union.

The government critics had a field day. Lemoux, the opposition leader from Quebec, held his own news conference. From his wheelchair he condemned the government and called on all fair-minded people to protest the government's stand. He left open just what form that protest should take.

The next day, we had more than our share of protestors ringing the studio grounds. If there hadn't been an equal number of people who supported us, it was doubtful that even the armed guards could have helped out. As it turned out, the provincial police were forced to come out and moderate.

Bridges and I were both late. We had gone straight to see Harway at the bank to straighten out the paper work. He was pleased that we had finally resolved the problems but not at all glad to see us. He was afraid the publicity might somehow spill over on the bank. In the end, greed won out. It was just too much money for his bank to turn away.

Pope had arrived at Kleinberg very early and had the whole place jumping. We learned at noon that the opposition under Lemoux had made a motion for a non-confidence vote. For the next two hours, we all waited while the government gathered every member of Parliament it could. One cabinet minister who had been speaking to the Toronto Chamber of Commerce was actually picked up by an air force jet and flown back for the stormy afternoon session.

When the vote was finally taken, the government managed to defeat the non-confidence motion by two votes. A slim margin but still enough for Devoir and his colleagues to remain in power. There had been the possibility that if the government had gone down in defeat, it would have taken our money with it. It was an outside chance, but still one that could have happened.

It didn't, and it looked like we were finally in the clear, financially at least. It was Bridges who proposed we hold the victory party. It was unanimously seconded. Clem Dunkin volunteered his loft. It was the only place downtown that any of us had that was large enough to accommodate all the people on the film.

The best news of all that day was from the hospital. Lenny Edwards was off the critical list and was expected to make a complete recovery. Dani and I went over to the hospital after the shoot and visited with him. He was still pretty grogged up, but all he was concerned about was whether or not he'd get his old job back. I'd already written up all his back checks and handed them to him. Then I told him he was on full salary for the rest of the production, whether he made it back or not. Under the circumstances, I told him, it might be better if he rested this one out.

Clem Dunkin's loft was a converted glove factory off of Spadina and College. The living room was a hundred feet by forty, and there were several rooms in the back that had once been offices but had been converted to living quarters.

The place was packed by the time Dani and I arrived. Everyone had brought something—food, wine, beer, liquor, and there was enough marijuana smoke in the air alone to have us all locked away for twenty years. But by and large it was an orderly party. To the best of my knowledge, there were only two people who didn't thoroughly enjoy themselves.

The first was Pope. I was on my way to the bathroom when I took a wrong turn and ended up lost in the maze of back rooms that Dunkin used for sleeping, painting, acting, eating, weight-lifting, and his other varied activities. I ran into Pope coming down the hall, so I asked him to direct me.

He had a terrible scowl on his face, which had been there for days. "Piss on yourself," was all he would say as he pushed by me and actually managed to shove me a little with his shoulder. I wasn't in any mood to fight, so I backed off and continued my hunt.

The next door I came to was slightly ajar. I looked inside and saw a couple in a warm embrace. Both were dressed and standing up, but it nevertheless caught me by surprise.

The couple was Catherine and Clem Dunkin. In spite of the fact that I knew about their supposed affair, it still kind of caught me off guard. I figured Pope had likely seen them a few seconds earlier.

They didn't see me, and I continued on my way and eventually found the bathroom. Where the line-up was, naturally. By the time I was done and had gone back out to the living room, Dunkin and Catherine were both there. Catherine was over in one corner, seemingly having a heated discussion with Pope. I couldn't hear what they were saying, as I was too far away, but from the way she was gesturing, it didn't look friendly.

Clem was in a different part of the room showing off his pratfalls for a couple of cute dollies that someone had brought to the party. He was the first and only person I had ever seen who could fall face down with his arms at his side and come up laughing. He managed it all by incredible muscle control, which allowed him to use his stomach and chest to absorb the shock of the fall and keep his face just a fraction of an inch off the floor. He gave the illusion his face was actually bearing the brunt of the fall. He'd showed me this one day at the studio during a break. He said it was easy and wanted me to try it. I decided to take his word for it and declined the offer.

The party went on for another two hours and might have lasted all night if Harold D. Kessler, the writer, hadn't made an unexpected appearance. He was the other person who didn't have a very good time.

He came in looking no more distraught than usual. At first he kept pretty much to himself and no one bothered him. He was drinking heavily and once passed me and managed a little smile. Somehow, I didn't expect it was really a friendly smile. I had a feeling he was up to something. I didn't have long to wait to find out what.

Shortly after one o'clock a fairly drunk Kessler ripped the wires out of the sound system. For a few moments, no one quite knew what was happening.

Then Kessler was on a chair in the middle of the room.

"Listen to me. Everybody. You've got to listen," he shouted. "You have to stop the picture."

Clem Dunkin moved fast. Faster than any of us. Dunkin literally plucked Kessler off the chair. Before anyone could even react, he was leading Kessler toward the door.

"Everything's going to be all right, Harold," Dunkin assured the soddened Kessler. "We'll just go outside for a little fresh air and talk about it."

Kessler walked along limply without protest until they reached the door. Then he broke from Dunkin and ran back into the center of the room.

"They're not going to let you finish it, don't you understand?" he shouted drunkenly.

Dunkin grabbed Kessler a second time. This time Kessler started swinging like a mad man. Dunkin did the only thing he could do under the circumstances. He floored the troublemaker. Kessler went down on his back and then slowly pulled himself to his feet.

Dunkin helped him up and walked him to the door. By the time he reached it, someone had plugged the stereo in again, and the music was again blaring through the loft. I worked my way through the crowd to the door. By the time I reached the street. Dunkin had just closed the door on a cab. It was pulling away with Kessler inside, slumped on the back seat.

Dunkin turned to me and tried a grin.

"Hey, why aren't you partying?" he asked.

I didn't say anything. We both walked back inside without saying a word. A small crowd greeted us at the door. Catherine had her coat.

"Everything's all right," Clem assured them.

"Maybe it's time we call it a night," Catherine said. "We all have to work tomorrow."

There was a feeble attempt by a few of the people to keep the party going, but no one really was in the mood. Twenty minutes later, the last of the guests were saying good night. Dani and I were among the last to leave.

In my wildest dreams I never would have imagined it would be the next to last time I'd see Clem Dunkin alive.

Chapter Thirty-Three

I also didn't expect to see Clem Dunkin less than two hours later. His phone call had brought me out of a deep sleep and I was more punchy than mad at him for waking me. On the other hand, I wasn't exactly pleased about being dragged out of bed. He was calling from a pay phone and said he was already on his way over but thought he should call first to get me up.

He thought he was being nice. I thought he was being a pain in the ass. When he finally walked through my door, doing what I thought was a drunk act, I was on the verge of getting mad. Until I saw the blood and realized the poor sucker had been shot.

The ambulance and the police both arrived at the same time. Their conclusion was unanimous. Clem Dunkin was dead. Dani was awake by this time. She sat solemnly on the couch beside the covered body and answered every question that was put to her in the same monotone. The two officers who came to investigate wanted to take us down to the station house, but I insisted they call Lieutenant Hagen.

Hagen arrived just as the morgue attendants were removing Dunkin's body. I felt a sense of relief when he took over the questioning. But that only lasted a few minutes until Brogan showed up. Hagen and Brogan got into a yelling match about who had jurisdiction. After a call in to the deputy supervisor, Hagen again had to bow out. Brogan had convinced the deputy supervisor that the murder could easily be part of a conspiracy stemming from the Flock of God people. His line of questions was directed in this channel. In the end, he marched us off to the station house.

Over the course of the night, he managed to pull in nearly everyone who had had contact with Dunkin during the last twenty-four hours. That, of course, included everyone who worked on the production, everyone who had attended the party, and all the people they had brought to the party. Hagen had gotten permission to sit in on the questioning but only as a spectator. Three hours passed before Brogan admitted that maybe this wasn't the work of the Flock of God people.

"I'm not saying it isn't," he warned everyone. "I think we have to have a little talk with Mr. Kessler first."

Kessler was one of three people at the party who, by morning, were unaccounted for. The other two were Pope and Catherine.

Just about everybody's first choice for a murderer was Kessler. He'd publicly threatened every one of us and had been punched out by Dunkin only hours before.

After Kessler, Pope made a pretty good runner-up. In hindsight, everyone on the production had seen or heard something that would indicate that he had been jealous to the point of rage that Catherine had been fooling around with Dunkin right under his nose.

I certainly didn't agree with Brogan's methods, but I did agree with him on one point. There was still a chance that it had been the Flock of God people. For my money, it could also be O'Shea and his pals. I suggested this to Brogan, but he snapped at me and told me to keep my mouth shut. To the best of my knowledge, he never did bother to investigate that angle.

I had a good mind not to tell Brogan about what Dunkin said, just out of spite. But in the end I had to for Dunkin's sake.

"Ten thousand what? Dollars? Peanuts?" Brogan looked at me coolly.

"I don't know. That's all he said," I explained.

"Thanks," he said, dismissing me with a wave of his hand. "If you think of anything else, don't forget to call."

It was nine o'clock by the time I got out of there. Actually they had finished with me three hours before. I had waited around for Dani. They had really put her through the wringer when they found out she had a record. She walked out with her head high.

When we got back to the hotel, she cried for an hour. We both slept for the rest of the day. I was awakened by the telephone about six. I'd left word at the desk not to put any calls through unless there was an emergency. I picked up the phone, expecting bad news.

It was Brogan on the other end. He wanted me to come down to the station right away. I asked him if it couldn't wait.

"Either you're down here in ten minutes or I send a squad car around with instructions to bring you in in bracelets."

Dani was still asleep. There was no sense waking her. I left a note where I'd be. On the way over to the station, I listened to the news. There was nothing new. The police investigation seemed to be zeroing in on the Flock of God people and Harold D. Kessler. Passing reference was made to the fact that Pope and Catherine St. Catherine had disappeared, but it wasn't suggested that this had any direct connection with Clem Dunkin's murder.

I arrived at police headquarters just under the ten minutes Brogan had given me. He kept me waiting an hour.

When I finally went in to see him he looked grim and ordered me to sit down.

I did. Then he reached into his desk and took out a box and opened it. Inside was a pistol that looked exactly like the one Bridges had brought by the hotel a few weeks before.

"You ever seen this before?" Brogan snarled.

"No," I said, shaking my head.

"You're a liar," he shot back. "It's got your prints on it."

I didn't say anything. It had to be the one Bridges had brought over. The one he swore he got rid of. As

172

for my fingerprints, I'd had a few run-ins with the law in my past. They'd have all my prints on file right there in the station house.

"Dunkin was killed with a .32 caliber bullet, the same kind as this gun," Brogan continued. "My boys found it on the back stairs an hour after Dunkin was murdered. I suppose you still don't have anything else to say."

I didn't move a muscle.

"All right," he said, "you can go."

I didn't have to be told twice. I headed for the door. There were a lot of questions running through my mind, but I just didn't feel like socializing with Brogan. Just as I reached the door, he called after me.

"Nevers."

I turned back slowly. He was holding the gun in the palm of his hand.

"I'm really disappointed, Nevers," he said. "I really thought I had you this time."

He laid the gun back on the table.

"There's only one trouble." he said. "This gun hasn't been fired in at least twenty years. You're lucky you ditched it when you did. If we'd found it in your room, we'd have dumped on you for illegal possession."

I nodded sullenly and left.

I called Dani and told her everything was all right and that I'd be a little while longer. Then I called Bridges. He was in his hotel, so I told him to wait and went right over.

It wasn't hard to get the information out of him. All I had to do was threaten to turn him over to Brogan. He came clean in a hurry.

He had given the other two guns away. One to Clem Dunkin. One to Pope. Clem could easily have gotten the one Bridges had originally handed me. Dunkin could have dropped it the night he was shot, when he was on his way up the stairs. It was just as likely that Pope had used the second gun on Clem, although I found that hard to accept. As for the other two guns, Bridges had them hidden, and not very well, in an old suitcase in the back of his closet. I checked both guns, and neither had been fired. One was actually so rusted there wasn't a moving part in it.

I wiped both clean and told Bridges I'd take care of them. I called Hagen and dropped by at his place. I explained how I had gotten the guns. He said he'd take care of disposing of them for me.

There was an outside possibility that Bridges had not given the fourth gun to Pope. Bridges had lied to me enough times before to make him suspect. There was always the chance that if there was a fourth gun, he himself had used it on Dunkin. But I found the whole idea of Bridges murdering anybody just too preposterous to think about. Still, I kept it filed in the back of my mind on the semi-active shelf.

Chapter Thirty-Four

I wasn't back at the hotel five minutes when Bridges called and said he'd gotten a threatening phone call from the Flock of God people.

"How do you know it was them?"

"They said so," he bleated.

"Have you called the police?"

"Yes, before I called you. They said they'd be right over."

"Call the security service and have a guard posted outside your room."

I didn't think he was in any real danger, but I knew a guard would make him feel better. He thanked me and hung up.

I met with Bridges the next morning at Kleinberg. The production was closed down, but we'd kept everyone on full pay in order to try to keep the continuity we'd need if we were going to finish the picture.

Bridges hadn't been the only one to get a threatening call. The cameraman and a couple of the minor players had also gotten calls. Everyone was noticeably shook over Dunkin's death, but at the same time there was a strange determination among the group to somehow finish the picture.

During the worst part of the money squeeze, Bridges had let two of the insurance policies lapse. The money that was available would only pay back less than half the money spent. If we pulled the plug, the Driscoll Corporation stood to take a million-dollar bath. On the other hand, they had signed the completion guarantee.

Bridges and I worked through the numbers before I got on the phone and started hunting down Schwarzer. There were a lot of contingencies to consider. Putting the disappearance of Catherine and Pope aside, and assuming they'd show up in a day or two, there would be the added cost of finding a replacement for Dunkin and reshooting all of the footage he had appeared in. Add to that the cost of the lost time and the extra guards and it came to an easy two million with another hundred thousand a day for each day we held off production.

Dani had moved in to Bridges's office and spent the whole day calling every agency on the continent looking for a replacement for Dunkin. The bad news was that no one wanted the part, no matter what the price. The only thing good so far to come from Dunkin's death was that the union pickets hadn't shown up at Kleinberg. Like vultures with nothing to pick over, they'd left us in peace.

It took me two days to reach Schwarzer through the number he had given me. He was calling from Detroit.

"I've been following your action in the papers, and I just want to tell you I've been rooting for you," he informed me. "Now, what can I do for you?"

I explained the situation to him briefly.

"Now, that is serious, my man." He sounded grim. "You just sit tight, and I'll call you as soon as I'm back in town."

The next morning Schwarzer showed up at the hotel. He had a car waiting downstairs, actually a chauffeur-driven limousine. We drove around on the expressways for about two hours, not going anywhere in particular from what I could tell, just up and down and back and forth. I filled him in on everything to date, including the fact that I knew about the Mosconi connection. He questioned me on every aspect of the film operation and made me go over and over the story several times until he was sure I hadn't left anything out.

He looked very thoughtful throughout. Finally,

after about two hours of cruising, he pushed the intercom button and spoke to the driver on the other side of the soundproof partition. He gave the driver a Mississauga address, sat back, and flicked a second button. A panel slid open and a small but adequate bar appeared.

"I think we're going to both need a little bracer," he said, pouring us two drinks.

The driver let us off in the Square One Shopping Center in front of Woolco. A second car, a blue Pontiac, picked us up. The second driver didn't need to be told where we were going.

"We don't like to ruffle the neighbors any more than we have to," Schwarzer said, referring to the fact that we had switched cars. The second driver took us to an ordinary-looking tract house in one of the newer housing developments that had sprung up in the area. It was a nice house but nothing unusual. There were three other cars parked along the curb or in the driveway. A blue Fiat sedan, a white Gremlin, and a maroon Pacer. It looked like your ordinary average bridge party.

Inside was cozy. The house had a woman's touch and had been lived in. I was brought into the recreation room in the basement where I was introduced to the three Mosconi brothers, Ronald, Alfred, and Benjy. It was Ronald's house. He apologized for the fact that his wife was on a vacation in Florida or he'd offer me lunch. I took a second drink instead.

The three brothers looked very much alike except for the fact that there was maybe five to seven years between them. Ronald, the eldest, had a few gray hairs and was balder and fatter than the other two. Benjy, the youngest, was the trimmest and was just beginning to thin out on top.

The three brothers faced Schwarzer and me across a coffee table in the middle of the rec room. Schwarzer gave them a few of the highlights, then they turned their attention on me. They made me go over my story from start to finish. I realized Schwarzer had made me go over it earlier so many times to make sure I wasn't lying. It soon was apparent that his head was on the block alongside mine.

When I finished, the three brothers started talking in Italian. I couldn't understand a word, but I realized the discussion had taken on a sharp edge. I tried to get some kind of indication from Schwarzer, but he stared stone cold ahead like he was some sort of statue.

The eldest brother, Ronald, finally explained for my benefit. They were, to say the least, unhappy with the latest turn of events, but they were also businessmen and understood that there were risks to any venture. He asked me what the bottom line was.

"If you want to cash in your chips now," I explained, "it'll cost you a million."

"What will it cost us to stay in?" Alfred, the middle brother, asked.

"Two million with a contingency of another five hundred thousand if we run over another week."

"What's the probablility you'll finish the film?" Benjy asked.

"At this point, it's impossible to say. The director and the leading lady are missing. We've got to find a new lead, and we have to reshoot about half of what we've already shot."

"It sounds like you're just about going to have to do another picture," Benjy observed.

I nodded.

"You're asking us to put up a lot of money on something that's pretty speculative even by your own evaluation," Ronald said.

"Look, Mr. Mosconi," I said, speaking to Ronald mostly, "you fellows have been looking for legitimate ways to invest your money. Maybe it isn't the best deal in the world, but it's legit. And if it does come off, you stand to make one hell of a lot of money. Ask Schwarzer if you don't believe me."

Schwarzer nodded affirmative.

I went on for several minutes, singing the virtues of the picture and explaining how I'd gotten into it as a tax shelter with the potential of bringing me in a bundle.

When I was finished, all three brothers shook my hand. Ronald said he would contact me after they had made their decision.

I left the same way I had come in, except this time Schwarzer wasn't with me.

At eight fifteen that evening he called me at the hotel and asked me to meet him on the corner of Bay and Queen in fifteen minutes.

I arrived on time. He picked me up in the same limousine I had ridden in earlier in the day.

"It's up to you," he said.

"I don't understand," I said, puzzled.

"The brothers voted and agreed that whatever you decided, they'd go along with."

"You mean they want me to make the decision on whether they take a million-dollar bath now or risk another two or three on the picture. Why, that means they'll be into the picture for five million before this is over."

"You were very convincing, Mr. Nevers," he assured me. "In either case, they've decided to hold you personally responsible for whatever happens."

Being personally responsible for five million dollars of the Mosconis money meant that if it didn't work out to their satisfaction, I'd be swimming Lake Ontario with concrete flippers.

Chapter Thirty-Five

I had no choice but to take the two and a half million. I was already responsible for a million of Mosconi money with no hope in hell of paying it back unless I completed the film and unless the film was a success.

I made it conditional just the same. I didn't have a lot of bargaining power. On the other hand, I had to assume that in the long run the Mosconis would rather make money than see me dead.

"There's a guy named O'Shea. He's head of Local 801w."

Schwarzer nodded. "I know who he is."

"Keep him off my back," I told him.

"I'll see what I can do."

It wasn't exactly a firm commitment, but it was the best I was going to get. We shook on the deal.

"I'll make sure the money's in your account by the end of the week," Schwarzer advised me.

I thanked him.

"One more thing," he went on, "I shouldn't be telling you this, but it wasn't a unanimous decision to go with you. Benjy wanted to write off the million and sink you in the lake. He thinks you're going to try to screw them. If you disappeared in the next few weeks, he'd be able to say 'I told you so.' My advice to you is to keep your eyes open."

I thanked Schwarzer again. He dropped me on the corner of Bay and Bloor. He was trying to help me for his own selfish reasons, but nonetheless it was meant as good advice. If I did manage to come out on top, I'd make him look good. If Benjy had me knocked off in the interim to make himself look good, then Schwarzer might find himself in a pretty weak position with the other two brothers.

The money was a boost to the old spirits but not much when I considered the fact that I had practically a whole movie to reshoot. I had no lead male. The leading lady and director were both missing. If that wasn't enough, I had no script, only a brief outline. Pope had kept the script under lock and key since the beginning. He'd taken the script with him when he'd disappeared.

The next day was Clem Dunkin's funeral. Everyone from the production showed up, as did a large representation of local celebrities. Devoir flew in from Ottawa as the government's representative. It was a highly unusual gesture, but he did it because of the government's involvement in the controversial affair.

He made a special point of avoiding the press, despite the opportunity to make political hay. He buttonholed me after the ceremony and asked if he could speak to me in private. I joined him in the back seat of his limousine. Dani chatted with the driver and Devoir's bodyguards by the front bumper.

"We've had our differences, Mr. Nevers," he told me, "and I know you don't personally like me."

"I don't like to be jerked around," I told him.

"We're in this together now. I won't be jerking you around, so perhaps we can bury the hatchet," he said, offering his hand.

"Fair enough," I said, shaking his.

"It's such a damned waste to see a man like Clem Dunkin gunned down because he was willing to fight for what he believed in. When you're in government you know the risks all too well. There's always someone who's unhappy with the way you do things, no matter what you do.

"I'm telling you all this," he went on grimly, "because what happened to Dunkin scares me. When the press asks me about assassination, of course I can't tell them I'm scared. I have to make up some acceptable

181

line, like I haven't time to think about that sort of thing. But I do think about it. I don't know a politician who doesn't, at least sometimes."

"Mr. Minister, if it's any consolation to you, I'm kind of scared myself these days," I admitted.

"We're all sitting targets, Mr. Nevers. Including Lazlo. I'm truly scared for him, too."

"I can understand your concern."

"If and when he should contact you, please call me immediately. He'll probably need help."

"All right," I agreed.

"I just wanted you to know I'm on your side."

We shook hands again, and he handed me his card with his private number on it. I thanked him and got out of the car.

I told Dani about the conversation.

"Maybe he's not so bad," I said. "Maybe he's got a pretty rough job after all."

Clem Dunkin's death had softened me. Dani was more skeptical.

"Let's see what happens when you need him."

I hated to admit it, but she was right.

There was still no word on Kessler, Pope, or Catherine. I dropped Dani off at the hotel. She had some woman's business to look after.

I drove up to the studio myself. It was kind of lonely. The only people around were the security guards. I stayed most of the afternoon looking over the figures. I spoke to Bridges about five. He was in the downtown office and had been calling Los Angeles most of the afternoon to see if he could find a replacement for Dunkin. So far it was still no luck. Because of the time difference, he was going to hang in a few more hours.

I finished off around six, said good night to the security staff, got in my car, and drove off.

I had left the studio compound and was only a mile along on the country road leading past the village of Kleinberg. There was a camper parked beside the road with its flashers on. A woman was standing beside the truck, trying to flag someone down. There weren't many cars on the highway that time of night. I wasn't in a hurry, so I pulled over. The woman was in her thirties and pretty in a kind of Dolly Parton way. She seemed quite upset.

"What's the trouble?" I asked.

"I don't know." She shook her head. "It just conked out on me. I've been trying to get it started for fifteen minutes."

"I'll have a look," I said, walking toward the camper with her. "You get in and turn the key."

She got in the cab, and I looked under the hood. Just as I did, I sensed something behind me. I turned to see O'Shea and two of his bigger pals from Local 801w walking toward me.

Just then, I heard the engine on the camper start up with no trouble at all. I'd been set up nice.

O'Shea and his two buddies moved in a half circle, forcing me to take them head on or move backward away from the camper and toward the field beside the road. I chose the latter.

O'Shea pulled the hood down on the camper and the driver leaned her head out.

"Everything all right, baby?" she asked O'Shea.

"Just fine, honey. You did just fine. Now, high-tail your little ass out of here, sweetheart."

She did what she was told. She drove off, leaving me to face O'Shea and his gang of two. I could have tried to run, but I'd have had a half a mile of open field going uphill before I reached any kind of cover.

It was dark, but the full moon and the snow would throw enough light to make me an easy target if they had guns.

I figured my best chance was to stay as close to the road as possible and hope that someone would come by. The only car in sight was mine. When I looked across the road after I'd been backed up a little farther, I saw a second car parked nose-in on a little dirt road about a hundred and fifty feet away. I figured it was their car. They'd been waiting across the street for me to stop. It would have been easy for them to spot me coming. Behind me from the top of the ridge, you could see the whole valley, including the studio. By the time

I got up the studio road, they'd have had plenty of time to get in position.

O'Shea and his boys circled me slowly, tightening the circle as they went. I wasn't exactly thrilled by my prospects, but I was starting to get the idea that they weren't out to kill me, just rough me up.

"I don't like people messing with my territory, Nevers. That was a bad move sending those guineas around. All it did was make my Irish blood boil," he informed me.

The other two just nodded.

"Just to show you how much I listen to what they have to say, I've come out here to redecorate your face," he continued as he moved closer. "The next time you see your wop friends you can tell them O'Shea did it."

With that he swung his big meaty fist at me. The second and third followed right behind. I tried to defend myself, but he had the movements of a boxer. His punches had the impact of heavy artillery. I felt my left cheek go dead. If I'd caught that one on my nose I'd be wearing it inside out. I couldn't fight this bastard on his terms. I was on the verge of being turned into hamburger. On top of that, while they seemed to imply that they wanted me alive, I had no guarantee they'd know when to stop. Under the circumstances, I did the only thing I could.

I gave O'Shea a swift kick that sent his kneecap halfway up his thigh. I followed that with a quick shot in the balls. When I was growing up, that would have been fighting dirty. I was grateful karate and judo had come along in the meantime. They'd legitimized kicking and biting.

I started yelling and screaming like a streetcar on a slippery track. I must have been pretty convincing. I was lucky as hell no one had bothered to bring along a gun.

The two thugs picked O'Shea up under the arms and started dragging him toward their car.

"I'll kill you, you bastard," O'Shea coughed. He sounded like he was crying. I took off on the run to my own car, started it up, and drove off before they got O'Shea across the road.

184

When I got back to the Ritz, Dani immediately wanted to know what had happened. I tried to laugh it off. She practically dragged me over to the mirror. I didn't have much feeling in the left side of my face, and and my ear was still ringing, but I hadn't realized the damage. I had the beginnings of two black eyes and a left cheek that could have hidden a basketball.

Ice and tender loving care couldn't make it all better, but it helped.

Chapter Thirty-Six

The next day the numbness was gone. In its place was a monumental headache. It would have been a good day to stay in bed, but I had some things to look after in Ajax. I drove out.

Jane Willson was pretty concerned, but I closed myself in the back office and worked over the books. Her new designs were coming in under budget, and I was working through the numbers to make a decision on whether or not to increase the building crew. I knew Jane would endorse a full nightshift, but I had to weigh the problem against the strain it might put on her. I didn't want her working day and night. On the other hand, if the plant went into operation sooner, I'd show black ink sooner.

It took me longer than I'd expected to go over the books. My mind kept wandering. It was nearly four in the afternoon when I finally called Jane in to discuss the proposal.

She took one look at me and insisted I needed to see a doctor. I told her to sit down. She wouldn't and kept nagging until I finally took a look in the mirror to see what she was excited about. My left pupil was the size of a dime. The right was a pinhead.

She drove me to the hospital and waited while the doctors fingered me and developed their X-rays.

The diagnosis—a concussion. The prescription—overnight in the hospital for observation. I wouldn't hear of it. I made Jane drive me back to the plant. She was so mad at me she wouldn't discuss the proposal, so I left and told her I'd come out the next day to talk it over.

"If you're not dead," she said.

A cheery lady when you got right down to it.

I drove toward the hotel, keeping my eyes out for O'Shea and his boys. I hadn't mentioned the incident to the police because I figured it would be pretty hard to prove. O'Shea had a whole union full of witnesses who'd swear he wasn't within forty miles of Kleinberg in the last week.

As I approached the entrance of the underground garage I heard a sharp crack. A second later there was a pressure on my eardrums like I was coming down in a jet.

The glass on the driver's side didn't break. The bullet tore through the glass and had buckled it, causing the pressure on my ears, but it had snapped back in place, leaving a hole the circumferance of my pinkie and a design that any spider would have been proud of.

I pulled the car into the garage. My first thought was Dani. I don't know why. Maybe it was the concussion. Maybe I was just plain scared. For both of us. I ran up the back stairs and into the room.

"You okay?" I asked as soon as I saw her, knowing it must have seemed like a dumb question to ask someone who is obviously okay.

She nodded but looked rather grim herself. She couldn't have known about the ambush. As it turned out, she didn't. She had her own piece of bad news.

Bridges had phoned five minutes before. Someone had sneaked through security and set fire to the studio. Bridges was on his way to Kleinberg, and he wanted me to meet him there.

I started to leave. Dani wanted to go too. I insisted she stay.

"For the first time in my life, I'm scared, really scared," she said. "Whatever happens, I want to be with you."

She told me that she'd received a threatening call right before the call from Bridges.

"Did they say who they were?"

"No." She shook her head. "Just 'Stop the movie or you'll die.'"

I reluctantly agreed to take her. She was probably no more safe at the hotel than with me. The bullet hole in my window didn't do much to give either of us a sense of security as we drove out to Kleinberg. She sat close to me with her left hand resting lightly on my right thigh. My hand rested on top of hers trying to assure her everything was all right.

There were at least four factions out there somewhere who would like to see me dead or out of action. Harold D. Kessler, Donald O'Shea, Benjy Mosconi, and the Flock of God people. And those were just the ones I knew about. I didn't discount the possibility that there could be others, directly or indirectly or not at all connected, who wouldn't mind me as worm food. Whoever was out there trying to get me knew they could probably do a faster job by getting to Dani first. I had no doubt that despite her innocence, they, whoever *they* were, would have no moral qualms about dragging her in.

When we reached the studio, the place was overrun with provincial police, media, firemen, and spectators. Nobody seemed to be in charge. Vehicles were parked all over the lot. We had to park on the edge of the compound and walk a good city block to the main buildings. The offices looked okay. Black smoke was coming out of the windows of the main studio behind the offices. The action was centered around that building. The firemen were pumping water into the building from all directions. The water made the ground soft and muddy in spots before it refroze in brown-white nodules of ice and mud.

Bridges was standing on the edge of the ring of firemen with his hands in his pockets.

"How bad?" I asked.

"It could have been worse," he mumbled. "It looks like they'll save the studio. Two of the main sets are gone. Most of the equipment and about three quarters of the props are okay. The security guards caught it just after it started."

"Arson?"

"Looks that way. They found a couple of empty

cans of gas on the other side of the main building. All in all, I think we'll come out of this okay. It's almost under control now."

"What's it going to do to the production?"

"With a double crew of carpenters we could rebuild the burned sets in ten days. In the meantime, we could shoot around them, provided of course that Catherine and Pope show up and we get a replacement for Dunkin," he said, then added, "And provided we don't have any more trouble."

"Let's hope so," I agreed.

"Billy, maybe this isn't the time to bring it up, but I got another one of those funny phone calls from the Flock of God people," Bridges told me. "It has me worried."

"Did you tell the police?"

"Yes. Someone came over, wrote down what I had to say, and said they'd be back to me. Quite frankly, I'd feel one hell of a lot better if I still had my gun. I'm sorry I gave it to you."

I knew he was better off without it, but there was no sense arguing the point.

We watched the firemen for the next hour while they hosed down the building until the fire was completely out. We went inside the building to inspect the damage. The firemen's initial reports had been accurate. There was slightly less structural damage to the building than they'd originally thought and slightly more water damage.

During the last hour, most of the police, media, spectators, and firemen had drifted off. Only a small crew of firemen and our own security force were still left when we finished our tour. Dani and I started toward the car.

Bridges asked me if I'd mind going to the office with him to sign some checks to get the clean-up started early the next morning. He offered to make us coffee, but Dani said she'd just as soon get started back to town as soon as I was finished. She hadn't said much the whole evening but I could tell the fire had given her the creeps.

To speed things, she said she'd warm the car up. I tossed her the keys and went inside the office with Bridges.

I started to sign checks when the building was rocked by a tremendous explosion which blew out all the windows. But it wasn't the office that had been hit. I ran outside.

My car doors were both open and the hood was on the roof. Dani was sitting in the driver's seat. She just looked at me and began to cry. Both her legs had been blown apart. The bones were sticking through in a dozen places. Part of the steering column had impaled her in the chest.

Her hands were still clutching the steering wheel, which had broken off from the impact. One of the firemen reached us a second later and together we tried to free her from the wreck. We finally had to use blowtorches.

It took us nearly forty-five minutes to cut her loose. By then the ambulance and a doctor had both arrived. Dani was conscious the whole time. They were afraid to dope her up because she needed all her strength to fight the beating she had taken. She kept saying over and over again, "Billy, I'm sorry, Billy, I'm sorry."

In between were the most horrible screams I have ever heard or ever want to hear again in my life.

I rode to the hospital with the ambulance. The doctor had pulled me aside and had tried to prepare me for the worst.

"There's no chance," he told me grimly.

Dani fought like hell. I stayed right there with her the whole time. Through emergency and up to surgery, where I watched from the amphitheater overlooking the operating room. In the end, it was too much for her. She died just before sunrise. A nice day. No clouds, a kind of pinkish purple sky that would turn into bright blue, her favorite color.

Chapter Thirty-Seven

When someone dies it takes a while for it to sink in. Even if you've seen it happen. I went back to the hotel. Her kimono was still neatly folded over the back of a chair. Her women things were still spread out on top of the dresser. There was still a lingering smell of her perfume in the suite. How the hell could she be here yesterday and gone today?

I knew then how Al Pacino had felt in the *Godfather* movie when his Italian girlfriend was killed by the dynamite-wired car. But he had Diane Keaton to go home to. I had no one. This wasn't a movie. It had really happened.

Why had it all happened? Why this way? That bomb had been meant for me. I was sure of that. Dani had saved my life. Without her, life just wouldn't be the same. If I had only stayed in the hospital overnight, if I had insisted she stay at the hotel, if I had gone to the car, if I'd pulled the plug on the film when Dunkin got killed, if, if, if . . .

I tortured myself with all the possibilities of what could be. I went around and around in circles. It was Jane Willson's call that snapped me out of it. She called to say how sorry she was.

"It's just horrible, Billy," she said, her own voice choked with emotion, "but at least they've caught him now."

"Caught who?" I asked.

"Harold D. Kessler. I heard it on the radio not more than ten minutes ago. They've caught that writer fellow in a downtown warehouse and are trying to get him to come out."

I thanked her for the information and hung up. I called police headquarters. Hagen and Brogan were both out. So was half the police force. Kessler had been spotted about an hour before in an abandoned warehouse near the lakefront. The first two policemen who had tried to enter the building had been gunned down.

I hopped into a taxi and took off for the waterfront address the desk sergeant had given me. I was stopped several blocks away. I had to get out and walk, but each time I tried to get close, I was turned back. I could hear small arms' fire in the direction of the warehouse and bullhorns shouting instructions back and forth. Two armed forces helicopters hovered overhead.

I finally located Lieutenant Hagen. He had set up his headquarters about two blocks from the warehouse and was directing his men from there. Brogan had his headquarters across the street.

One of Brogan's men had spotted Kessler just around the time Dani had died. He had reported it, and Brogan had come down with a dozen squad cars. He had led a group of his men into the building but had been driven back by machine-gun fire, which had killed two of his men. He called for more reinforcements, but by the time they arrived, the Royal Canadian Mounted Police in association with the armed forces had moved in and claimed jurisdiction because the warehouse was on federal property. They had pushed the city police back to where Hagen and Brogan had set up their offices.

"We're trying to get a reading on what's happening, but they won't tell us a thing," Hagen said, shaking his head.

Just then, one of Hagen's officers came in to tell us the building Kessler was in was on fire. We ran outside and could see smoke and flames from the street. We tried to get closer but were stopped by a ring of soldiers in battle gear.

They wouldn't let the city fire trucks through either. The Mounties and soldiers made absolutely no attempt to stop the fire themselves. Several loud explosions rocked the area from the warehouse building and were presumed to be caches of dynamite stored inside. Presumed because the Mounties and military jointly slapped a tight lid over any information coming out of the siege front.

As the day went on, more and more military vehicles arrived and the city police were moved farther and farther away from the area. The skyline was black with smoke by early afternoon. By six o'clock that night the building had collapsed and was burning itself out.

The first reports that were jointly issued by the Mounties and military said a body had been found and tentatively identified as that of Kessler, and by ten o'clock it had been positively identified from dental charts.

By the following morning, no new light was shed on the affair. The military vehicles were gone. So was the warehouse. The entire building had been scraped clean and hauled away. The city police issued a communiqué that said Kessler had rented the wooden building nearly a year and a half before under another name.

I went to see both Hagen and Brogan, but neither could give me any additional information.

"Officially, we can't be sure," Brogan told me, "but unofficially, we're betting that Kessler killed Dunkin and Miss Davis. Everything points to it. Even the Mounties think so."

I just couldn't buy that. Not that easily. I pushed him for details on why the military had moved in on the area and slapped a blanket over all information.

"That's the way the military works. They go on a picnic and it's top secret."

"I don't believe that. And you don't either, if that's all you know."

"They have their reasons. That's all I can say," he insisted.

"You can't say anything because you don't know any more. They tell you to jump and you ask how high," I said, trying to get him mad enough to maybe take some action on his own.

"Look, Nevers, if you're so interested in looking in

closets, I suggest you start looking in your own first before you come in here and start telling us how to run our business."

"You're not going to put me off that easy," I told him angrily. "I don't have anything to hide."

"You might just be dumb, or you might be lying through your teeth, but either way, I'm going to do you a big favor."

"What's that?"

"We know all about Michael Jon Bridges and Benjy Mosconi."

I looked at him cockeyed. "What you talking about?"

"The Mounties got a tap on the phone between those two. They're so close they're practically lovers."

Chapter Thirty-Eight

There was nothing more to say. I left. I had this gut feeling that nothing had been resolved by Kessler's death. He was just one small pipeline in the sewer I was walking around in. If Dani were still alive, I would have packed my bags and taken her as far away from the city as I could and never looked back. But she was dead. I felt half dead myself. But now there was no reason to run. I was going to find out what was going on if it was the last thing I ever did.

The information Brogan had given me on Bridges and Mosconi threw a whole new light on everything. If Bridges had been in with Mosconi from the beginning, it was possible he was in on the conspiracy to kill Dunkin.

He'd been a child impersonator. Was it Bridges who had made all those phone calls that had come from the Flock of God people? Had he and Mosconi killed Pope and Catherine? Where did O'Shea fit in? Why was there so much mystery surrounding Kessler's capture? Who the hell else was involved?

Two things struck me as peculiar. First, Brogan kept a tight lip on the Kessler incident but easily dropped the fact that the Mounties were investigating Bridges and Benjy Mosconi. He wanted me to know about that. But why? Second, he didn't make any mention of the fact that I'd seen the Mosconis and had an association with Schwarzer. If they knew about Bridges, then they must have known about me, too. If they didn't want me to know, it was because I looked like good bait.

If they were following me, then how come no one showed up when there was trouble. It tweaked my craw that someone from the law enforcement community might have been within shouting distance when O'Shea did his business on me but had orders to let nature take its course.

There was still another possibility. Brogan might have really been offended by my insults and been shooting off his mouth. There was a remote possibility that everyone except me really believed the Kessler theory—that Kessler had done it, and now that he was gone, things would get back to normal. There were grounds to support that theory too. For one thing, no one had bothered to conduct much of an investigation of the explosion that had killed Dani. No one had even interviewed me, unless you wanted to count the five minutes I spent talking with the responding officer at Kleinberg after the incident happened.

The last thing I wanted to do right then was make movies. On the other hand, I figured it was the only way to smoke out what was really happening or forever satisfy myself that all the loose ends really were loose ends. Kessler had been the sole bad guy.

My first stop was Bridges. I didn't soft-shoe around.

"I'm sorry about Dani," he said when I walked through the door at the downtown office.

"Bullshit, you're sorry. You tell me about you and Benjy Mosconi."

"I don't know what you're talking about."

Not likely, I thought. The little grub had turned a deathly white. I grabbed him by the collar and walked him to the window.

"You start talking or you're going downstairs," I said in a firm, steady voice, "and you're not taking the elevator."

I hadn't slept in two days and I was still popping aspirin to deaden the effects of the concussion. My face was a blue-yellow-purple from O'Shea's handiwork, so I definitely looked the part I was acting out.

Bridges didn't need a lot of coaxing. He started talking and talking fast. So fast in fact that little bubbles of spit formed on the corners of his mouth and gave him the image of a tired old dog.

Yes, he knew Benjy Mosconi. Yes, he had been in contact with him about a film deal. No, it didn't have anything to do with *Crash*.

"For God's sake, Billy, in this business you're only as good as your next film." Bridges wrung his hands. "I swear it had nothing to do with our business."

"But you are dealing with him," I insisted.

"Yes, on a possible three-picture package," he explained, "but for God's sake don't hold that against me. I need the money."

"Why?" I said. It was a strange question to be asking your partner after so long. It had occurred to me that Bridges must have made a fortune in his lifetime, yet he didn't seem to have much at any one point. I'd tried several times before to get him to open up, but he'd always sidestepped the question. This time he didn't.

"Have you ever heard of Eva Gazar?" he asked, taking a deep breath.

"You mean *the* Eva Gazar?"

"Yes." He nodded.

"Sure, I knew who she was. She was the most beautiful woman in films in the 1950s. I used to have the biggest crush on her. Then she stopped making movies. But what's this have to do with *Crash?*"

"Did you ever wonder why she stopped making movies?" he asked. His voice trembled slightly as he spoke.

I had, but then Howard Hughes had dropped out around the same time. I never thought of asking. Bridges explained.

"Because she didn't have to. Because in 1955 she married me, and I've given her all the money she's needed ever since," he told me.

"But she lives in Hollywood and you lived in . . ."

"Yes. You see, I was already married to a second woman, a showgirl from New York who wouldn't give me a divorce. There were children and it got messy. I ended up in jail, then jumped bail and left. I haven't been able to go back since. Eva comes to visit me twice a year no matter where I am. She stays a week each time, and at the end of the week, I give her everything I have. It's the sad old story of a sad old man, perhaps. But for anyone who's ever been in love, they must know that that week with her is the only part of my life that matters anymore."

Bridges walked away from me and sat down heavily in one of the chairs. I just stared at him, trying to figure whether I'd been treated to the largest shovelful of bullshit that had ever been scooped or whether I'd just met the last of the romantics. I actually found myself wanting to believe him. I couldn't believe he was really a bad guy. On the other hand, I had to find out what else he was hiding from me. What other scrap of information.

I quizzed him about his relationship with Mosconi. He went over the conversations again and again. It sounded like a straight business deal. Mosconi had come to Bridges with the idea of doing a series of films and setting up an old-style Canadian-based film factory. If it was true, there was still reason for Benjy to want to knock me off. He might have felt that he could control more of the action directly if he worked through Bridges. There were a number of questions about the internal workings of the Mosconi family that still drew blanks. We weren't getting anywhere on that line of thought.

I started working backwards, working Bridges over for every scrap of information he knew about the original film deal. I wanted to know everything I could about how he'd gotten involved, what Pope had been like when he had first approached Bridges, how Catherine and Pope had been together, what the relationship between Kessler and Pope had been like in the beginning, and anything else that he had observed or could infer.

I pumped him for two solid hours. I finally found the weak spot. It wasn't in anything he said, but in something he didn't say. Every time I'd get to the night Dunkin was killed, I'd notice more eye flicker than usual, and I was sure he was hiding something.

In the end, I wore him down. He was scared to

give me the information. He hadn't told the police or any-one else.

"The night Dunkin got murdered, he called me first," Bridges admitted reluctantly. "He said he had some important information, but I told him I didn't want to know. I told him to call you."

"Did he say anything, anything at all?" I asked.

"No, nothing. He said it was important but I said I didn't want to know," he said, shaking his head. "I suppose I could have told the police, but what difference would it have made?"

Bridges was still on a temporary visa and knew that any involvement with the police would prejudice his case for permanent residence status. He was worried that his chances had already been ruined.

"Think back," I told him. "Isn't there anything that anyone said or did that would throw some light on what Dunkin might have found out or why he would have called you."

"No, nothing." He shook his head.

But it was my turn to do some digging. When Dunkin had come in, he had said something to me. Something that no one had ever figured out.

"Does 'ten thousand' mean anything to you?" I asked.

Bridges looked blank and continued to shake his head.

"Think, man. Ten thousand dollars. Ten thousand feet of film. Ten thousand extras." I fished.

He looked up at me, and there was a frightened look on his face.

"Guns," he said. "Ten thousand guns."

"Guns, what guns?"

"I don't know exactly, but Kessler and Pope used to have a little private joke between them when they were working on the script back in the days when they were just getting the project off the ground."

"What did they say?"

"I don't remember exactly." Bridges strained. "But it was something they'd say to each other when some-

199

thing would go wrong. One would say to the other, 'Don't worry. Ten thousand guns says this picture is going to get made.' Or something like that."

"What does it mean?"

"I don't know."

"Did they say anything else?"

"No, nothing that I can remember."

"Ten thousand guns," I repeated to myself. "What the hell can that mean?"

"I don't know, I don't know," Bridges said wearily. "And I don't think I want to know."

"Did you ever see the script they were working on?" I pushed on.

"No. Pope came to me with the story outline. I could see what he had and I knew it would work. Pope had a well-structured treatment and a track record, and I knew I could sell that."

"That's all?"

"No. He'd been working on the project for a long time before he met up with me. He said he'd lined up some government money, but it was conditional on raising private funds. That's why he needed me."

"The government money was Devoir."

"Yes, in the beginning they were very supportive. They never hinted there would be any difficulties if we could raise the private money."

"So Devoir was in from the beginning."

"Yes. Whenever I'd go to Ottawa with Pope in tow, Devoir would see us. But I did notice one thing that puzzled me."

"What was that?"

"Devoir and Pope always seemed to have a certain friction between them, even when they were smiling at each other and slapping each other on the back. Maybe I was just imagining it, but I always felt there was some bad blood somewhere between the two of them. I never paid much attention though. All I wanted to do was make the damned picture."

Chapter Thirty-Nine

I kept at Bridges for another hour, but there was nothing more I could get out of him. He was empty. Or so I thought. There was still the possibility that he was lying and that he was in deeper than I'd like to believe, but for the time being, I was penciling him off the list.

I tried to get through to Devoir. He wasn't in, but he didn't keep me waiting. He called me right back.

He told me how sorry he was about Dani, then asked if I'd heard from Pope. When I told him no, he seemed disappointed.

I told him I wanted to know why the Mounties and the military had thrown up a security blanket around the Kessler affair.

"That's not my area, Billy. I really can't help you."

"But why?"

"I'm sure from what I do know, and from what I can say, that it had nothing whatsoever to do with Kessler per se but with the building and the location. That's all I can really tell you."

"You mean like strategic offices in the area or classified equipment stored in the vicinity?" I suggested.

"Something like that," he patronized me. "Now, if you should hear from Lazlo or Catherine, and I can be of any help, don't forget to call."

I got off the phone and had that funny feeling all over again in the pit of my stomach. I hadn't told Devoir what I had found out. And obviously he wasn't telling me what he knew. I knew I was sticking my neck out to pursue the facts, but what else could I do. Dani was dead. Somebody had killed her trying to kill me. It might not have been Kessler.

I went to see Lieutenant Brogan at police headquarters again. I told him I thought he was covering something up. He got mad and started yelling at me.

"The case is closed, Nevers. I got orders from the Mounties to turn over all our files. And that's it. Now get out of my office before I find something to charge you with," he bellowed.

"Where's your sense of justice and fair play?" I asked him, getting to my feet.

"Closed," he repeated.

"No, not closed," I insisted. "You were inside that warehouse with the police on the first wave. And you saw something, didn't you?"

"Out," he said, standing up and coming around the desk.

"I'll tell you what you saw. There were guns, lots of modern guns, but badly rusted like they'd been exposed to the weather a long time."

Brogan stopped a few inches from me. His lower lip twitched. "Where did you find that out?"

I didn't say anything. I just turned to leave. He grabbed me by my arm, spun me around, and slapped me against the wall.

"I want to know which one of my men broke security," he hissed. "You better tell me now. This could be a long federal problem for you if you don't."

"You told me." I eyed him coldly. "I was only guessing, but now I know."

Brogan raised his hand to wack me across the face. I pushed him back against his desk.

"If you're going to lay a hand on me, Brogan, you better kill me or make sure I never talk again. Because if anyone ever asks me how I found out, I'm going to tell them you told me. You're the one who broke security."

I left Brogan standing there not knowing which way to turn. I knew enough about the cop system to know that orders had come down from some very high place to the city police to stay out of the whole affair and let the Mounties and military handle it.

I was starting to get a pretty good idea why, but there were still a lot of little pieces that needed to be put together.

I stopped off at the *Toronto News* building and talked my way into the microfilm room. It took me about a half an hour to find what I was looking for. Two years before, almost to the day Dani had been killed, Kessler had written a story about a mysterious ball of fire sighted over Lake Ontario. The phenomenon had been sighted by a number of people on both sides of the border.

The fireball story might have gotten more coverage on an ordinary day, but another story had dominated the national news and pushed it to the second page. The front page was covered with the story of the shooting of opposition leader Pierre Lemoux, which had taken place the night before and only a few hours before the fireball had been sighted over the lake.

Lemoux's fight for life and the search for the assassin continued for several weeks, but no one ever followed up on the fireball story. Kessler left the *News* several months later to try his hand at film writing.

It was late when I finished at the *News*. I called the hotel to see if there were any messages. Bridges had called. I reached him at his hotel.

"We have a payroll to raise tomorrow," he reminded me. "We ought to start thinking about whether or not to wind the film down and take our chances."

"We draw the payroll tomorrow, and we keep on drawing it," I told him. "This film is going to get made, one way or the other."

I told him I'd stop in sometime the next day at the downtown office to sign the checks.

He invited me to have dinner with him. But I just didn't feel like eating. Instead I went to Kessler's last known address before he took up residence in the warehouse.

I found the building and discovered he'd moved out three months before and had taken everything with him, presumably to the warehouse where it had been burned and the ashes carted away.

I took a long shot and called all the Kesslers in the book. I got his mother on the fourth try. She didn't want to talk to me. She thought I was from the press.

I told her I was a friend of Harold's and that I might be able to prove his innocence, but only if I could see her and ask her some questions. She reluctantly agreed.

I had rented another car during the day and drove out to the address she gave me. It was a simple three-bedroom house tucked away in a corner of Don Mills. Mrs. Kessler lived alone with two cats. Her husband had died two years before of kidney failure and now Harold was dead. She told me all this while we sipped tea and sat on her plastic-covered sofas in the living room.

At first she started to cry every time I tried to talk about Harold. To her, he was such a good boy. Not the kind of boy who would ever get in trouble.

"Can you tell me anything about his friends?" I asked.

"He didn't have any friends. He lived for his writing. He told me someday he would write the great American novel. He was such a good writer and always working so hard," she said, then got to her feet and motioned for me to follow. "Come, I'll show you what I mean."

She took me to Harold's room. It was book-lined from floor to ceiling. She pointed out several trophies and plaques he had received in high school and college for outstanding scholastics and for various writing contests.

There was one trophy that caught my eye. I picked it up and looked at it more carefully. It had the figure of a male swimmer and it read: "Harold D. Kessler. Third Place. Breast stroke. Intercollegiate Junior Varsity Games. 1967."

"Was Harold a swimmer?" I asked.

"Oh, yes, and a very good one," she said. "But he didn't like competition in sports. He said he had enough competition in writing, so he never stuck with that part of it. He took up scuba diving instead."

She went on to tell me how he spent many week-ends diving in the Georgian Straits and in Lake Ontario, looking for old wrecks of ships.

"I used to worry about him a lot because he'd always go out alone. But then, young people, you can't tell them anything these days. They're all so smart." She sighed, then broke out in tears again.

I thanked her for her time and left, promising if my hunch about Harold was right, I'd be able to prove that he was innocent.

I got up early the next morning and met Bridges at his office to sign checks. He told me that he thought we should close down the operation, that he hadn't even gotten a nibble for the male lead. He'd also been looking for possible replacements for Catherine and even Pope, but no one wanted to know about the project. It was a Jonah. I again told him we were going to keep going and that was that. He said he'd do what he could.

"Even if we replace all the people, we still don't have a script," he reminded me.

"We'll write one if we have to," I told him. "But we're going to make this movie."

I left him with the bookkeeping and drove out to the airport to check one more hunch. I talked my way into the traffic controller's offices, using Lieutenant Brogan as my reference. I was pretty sure if they believed me they wouldn't check.

The office manager let me see the old records. I wanted to see the records for all commercial, cargo, and private plane flights out of the airport on the night the fireball had been sighted over Lake Ontario. When we looked through the record books, we found that those pages had been torn out.

"That's the first time I noticed this," the manager told me. "I don't know who would want this kind of information."

"Who else is likely to see these books?" I asked.

"Any one of a dozen people, or more." He shrugged. "We don't keep the old books under lock and key."

There was another set of records kept by the cargo outfits and he suggested I try there. I checked with

205

several cargo outfits and took copies of the flights out from their docks. I wasn't sure yet what I was looking for until I went to see National Cargo. It was a big outfit and they did a lot of work for the government. When I checked their books, I found the records missing for the night in question. The clerk who showed me the records confirmed that I was as close as I thought I was to something important.

"You know, we don't get much call for people going through these records," he told me. "The last time I remember anyone asking about them was maybe eighteen months ago, maybe more. It was that reporter fellow that got himself shot up in the warehouse downtown. I recognized his picture in the papers."

He meant Kessler. He was sure it was the same person. I thanked him and left. I had no doubt that it had been Kessler who had come out and looked over the records. It might have been Kessler who tore the pages out of the log books, or then again, it might have been someone else who came after him. My problem was I had a thin idea of a story line taking shape in my mind but not a single shred of evidence. I'd also run out of ideas on where to look. If Kessler was alive, he'd be able to fill in at least some of the blanks. I knew who had killed him, but I didn't know why. It occurred to me that the last coherent thing he had said at the party the night Dunkin was killed was "They're not going to let you finish the movie." Who were "they"?

Chapter Forty

I might have been forced to give up, despite my promises to Dani's memory. No matter how hard I tried, I probably would have gotten no further than I had already had gone if it hadn't been for one lucky break.

The next day was Dani's funeral. I was too numb to pay much attention to who was there and who wasn't. On first glance, most of the same people who had been at Dunkin's funeral were there, with the possible exception of Devoir.

I don't like funerals at the best of times. This was a particularly painful situation. I listened to the clergyman giving the blessing. I kept staring down at that box and saying this is all absurd. Dani can't be in there. She's at home at my place reading a book from back to front so she'll know how it all turns out.

Right in the middle of the ceremony I found myself getting dizzy and felt like the crowd was punishing me into the hole in the ground with her. I turned and pushed my way through the mourners and kept walking without looking back. As I got through the front ranks of people, the crowd thinned out. A number of people stood at some distance, observing the ceremony from afar.

People kept touching me and saying, "It's okay," or "I'm so sorry." I didn't want to hear any of that. I just wanted to get as far from there as possible. I kept my head down as I walked, so nobody could catch my eye. And I almost missed her because of that. If I had, there was every chance that, as I said, no one would ever have unraveled the truth.

She was standing beside a tall family monument. She was wearing a plain brown coat and a black wig. Her face was hidden by a veil and sunglasses. If she'd stayed put, I never would have noticed. But as I came toward her she must have thought I had recognized her, and she started to walk away. When she realized I hadn't, she stopped and took up a second position beside another large monument.

I gave the impression that I hadn't recognized her, but I knew that walk. It belonged to Catherine St. Catherine.

I walked up the hill and away from the action, out of sight of where she was standing. I didn't want to spook her, but I didn't know exactly how to approach her. I tried to circle back through the headstones. When I reached the spot where she had stopped the second time, she was gone. I was afraid I'd lost her. The ceremony was just about over, and more people were leaving the core of the crowd. I knew in a few minutes it would be impossible to get my car out.

I walked fast up to the top of the ridge again, figuring that she had also recognized the traffic problem and had probably decided it was the best time to leave.

I spotted her getting into a taxi at the bottom of the hill just as I reached the crest of the hill. I hurried to my own car and drove out of the cemetery after her.

I tried to keep my distance, but I'd already lost her once and didn't want to do it again. I just had to take a chance that she wouldn't see me.

The taxi let her off about three dollars worth from the cemetery on the fancy Bridle Path. I drove by and kept her in my rearview mirror until she was out of the cab and heading toward one of the houses.

It is one of those neighborhoods where no one walks around because there aren't any sidewalks. The houses are all set on large tracts, and anyone approaching from the front can be spotted before they are within a hundred yards of the house.

I'd hiked around that area when I was a kid before

it had been turned into housing tracts. I knew a ravine ran behind a couple of the houses, including the one Catherine had gone into.

I parked my car about a mile down the road and hiked back through the ravine. I was about two houses away and trying to figure how to sneak up on the house without being seen when a kid about ten came down the ravine and demanded to know, in a very loud voice, what I was doing back there.

"I'm visiting some friends." I smiled.

"This is our property and you shouldn't be on it," she insisted.

"I'll be off it in a second. So bug off," I told her, more annoyed at her posturing than anything else.

"We've had a lot of robberies in the neighborhood. I'm going to tell my mother you're back here," she yelled as she turned and headed for her own house.

For all I knew, whoever was in Catherine's house had already heard the commotion. In any case I gave the kid less than two minutes to reach her own house and drag her mother over to the telephone. I had to make my move whether I liked it or not. I climbed the edge of the ravine and tried to look as inconspicuous as possible as I moved across the lawn toward the back of the house Catherine had gone into.

As there was nothing worth hiding behind in the backyard, I was forced to make a beeline for the back door. I reached it without incident. I tried to see in the windows, but they were all heavily curtained. I saw the girl from two houses away coming out the back door of her house with her mother in tow. She started pointing at me.

When you're in the wrong there's only one thing you can do. Look like you know where you are and what you're doing. It doesn't work all the time, but it's better than panic.

I turned the knob on the back door. I opened the door and walked inside. I felt something hard hitting me across the back of the head. I remember wondering if it was bad for my concussion. Then I was gone.

When I woke up, I was tied to a fourposter bed—

spread eagled. There was a man about twenty-five sitting in the chair beside me. He looked at me and got up and left the room. I couldn't have said anything if I tried. My mouth was plugged with tape. I tried to hum through my nose to get someone's attention.

A minute later the young man returned with none other than the Reverend Davidson Smith in all his bearded glory. Catherine's father sat his huge frame down on the edge of the bed beside me and stared hard into my eyes.

"If you promise not to yell, I'll remove the gag," he told me.

I nodded, and in one quick motion he tore the tape from my mouth, taking most of my face hair with it.

"Now, what's all this about?" I asked as innocently as I could.

"You've come here to make trouble for us. I'm afraid we have no choice but to keep you a prisoner or kill you."

I realized the former was a real prospect. I didn't really think they had killed anyone. It wasn't in their credo. They were destroyers of property and quite possibly had dynamited Ajax and set fire to Kleinberg and sent around the death threats, but I couldn't believe in the final analysis that they had killed Dani or Clem.

"I came to see Catherine. I know she's here. I just have to talk to her. I have no interest in you or the members of your church."

"Catherine has returned to the flock. Is Lazlo Pope here, too?" I asked. "I think it's best if you don't try to talk to her."

He didn't answer. He didn't have to. Catherine came into the room a second later. Smith's eyes burned, and he shot her an angry glance.

"I told you not to come down here," he scolded her, but it was the voice of a father just the same.

She ignored him and immediately came over to me.

"I heard you had come to," she said, untying my wrists. "You shouldn't have come here," she pouted, then added, "You'll only make it worse for all of us."

The Reverend Smith watched her untie my hands

and said nothing. The young man also stood by the door and said and did nothing.

"You brought Pope here, didn't you?" I said.

"Yes." She nodded.

"I must see him."

"He's not well."

"I have to."

She nodded like she understood. When she finished untying me, she got up and left the room. I followed her out. Neither the Reverend Smith nor the young man made any attempt to stop me or follow.

'I might as well tell you, Billy," Catherine spoke as she led me down the hall of the large rambling house, "Lazlo tried to commit suicide by cutting his wrists when he heard about Dani. He's very upset and he blames himself."

"Did he say why?"

"No, he won't tell anyone. My father had you tied up because he was afraid you would try to hurt him."

"You don't think I will?" I asked.

"Not on Dani's account, because I can tell you for sure he didn't do it. He was here with me the whole night."

"I know he didn't do it," I told her, "but there are a few things that he can still help me with."

"You can try," she said, "but if you don't get anywhere, do I have your word that you'll leave and forget you were ever here?"

"Yes." I nodded.

She led me down a stairway to a small den on the ground floor. There was a fire burning brightly in the fireplace. Pope was sitting in a rocking chair staring out the window.

"Lazlo, Billy's here to see you," Catherine said softly.

Pope got up and slowly turned around to face me. He had aged ten years. He had a dazed look in his eyes, but he didn't look all the way gone. I thought I could probably shock him back into reality if I played my story right. I was just hoping that if the going got rough, Catherine would stick in there and not fall apart on me. She didn't look in the best of shape either.

"Where's the script?" I demanded.

He just looked at me.

"I want the script, Pope," I insisted, giving my voice just a slight edge of meanness that can be a whole lot more effective than yelling. "You give me the script, and I'll get out of here."

Pope looked at me and his mouth twitched. He was expecting something completely different. He was glad as hell to get rid of me so easily. He walked to his briefcase in the corner of the room and took out a neatly bound hundred pages and handed the manuscript to me.

I took it and flipped through the pages. I could see the character names of the IRA members, the British secret service, the Nazis, and the other characters of the King George assassination script.

"Not this one," I said. "The other one."

Pope just stared at me with fear in his eyes.

"Where is the other script?" I demanded.

Catherine looked from Pope to me and back again. It was all new to Catherine but not to Pope. He knew exactly what I was talking about.

"I know about the other script," I told him. "Now where is it?"

"There isn't any other script," he said quite unconvincingly. He sat down wearily in an armchair and stared at me. I sat down opposite him.

"Let me tell you what I know," I said. "Then you tell me if there wasn't another script. The one that you and Kessler first wrote and took to Devoir."

I began the story and he listened nervously. When I was done, he asked me who else knew.

It was Catherine who spoke first. "You mean what Billy's just said is true?" she asked, dumbfounded.

"Yes." He nodded, then asked me again who else knew. I told him no one as far as I could tell. I'd guessed what had really happened.

The discussion was like a catharsis of sorts for Pope. He looked relieved, and instead of retreating into his shell, he proceeded to elaborate on the story I had told him. He told me a number of details that I couldn't have found out, but which Kessler had discovered when he was researching the story.

"Dani, Dunkin, and Kessler are dead because of it," Pope said with a great sigh of resignation. "There's not a damned thing that any of us can do about it. You're like me now, Billy. If they ever find out you know, you're a dead man too."

He pulled up his sleeves and showed me the bandages on his wrists. "I tried to kill myself," he explained, "because I couldn't stand waiting around for them to get me. And they will. Maybe not right away. But in a week or a month or a year or two. They'll get you too if they know you know."

"Can't we do something?" Catherine asked.

"We can try," I told both of them.

Chapter Forty-One

Pope had been telling the truth about the King George assassination script being the only one. He had destroyed the original script. I had a lot of trouble convincing him that he had to rewrite the original one from memory. In the end it was Catherine who convinced him. She explained that she'd been carrying on with Dunkin for only one reason. To get Pope to act like a man. Despite all the gossip, she hadn't been sleeping with Dunkin.

"I love you and I have always loved only you," she told him. "I'll go on loving you forever. But I can't go on forgiving you forever."

She told him he had to write the script or she'd leave him for good. In the end, he rolled up his sleeves and got down to business. I called Bridges and told him not to worry and not to send the police looking for me. I didn't tell him where I was, but I told him I was okay.

Pope turned out nearly twenty pages a day. I stayed right there and watched it come out of the typewriter. It took six days to complete. When it was done, I called Devoir and told him I wanted to have a meeting with him. He said he was terribly busy, but I insisted. I told him just enough to let him know that I might be on to him, and finally he agreed to see me the next day.

The next morning I was in his office at ten o'clock. He didn't seem pleased to see me. I handed him the manuscript that Pope had typed up.

"What's this?" he asked, fingering the script.

"It's a movie that I think you might be interested in," I told him.

"I haven't got time . . ." he started to say.

"I'll tell you the story if you don't have time to read it," I cut him off.

His eyes smoldered as he looked at me.

"I'll give you five minutes to tell me what this is all about," he said, looking at his watch.

I began my story.

"Just over two years ago a reporter by the name of Harold D. Kessler was sent out on a story to cover a mysterious fireball sighted over Lake Ontario. He did a good job on the story, but it got pushed to the second page, because that same night there was an assassination attempt on the Premier of Quebec. The end result was that Pierre Lemoux was gunned down and left paralyzed for life.

"Kessler might have forgotten about his story except for two things. He checked with the planetarium and found out there was no evidence of any meteorite in the skies that night. Secondly, he didn't believe in UFOs. He started doing some digging on his own. He started piecing together an incredible story.

"By springtime when the waters were warm enough, he took a little skin-diving expedition into the lake and with a little bit of luck actually found the spot where the fireball had gone down. What he found on the bottom confirmed what he had discovered.

"Several months before, the NATO allies had approached the Canadians with a scheme that they believed would capture Santos Montenegro, the Argentine medical student turned terrorist who has the highest number of kills attributed directly to him of any terrorist in modern history.

"Montenegro had been active in seeking a new pipeline for guns for the Red Brigade at the time. The Canadian military, through a network of intermediaries, had approached him and said that Canada might look the other way in a gun-smuggling operation, provided Santos was willing to carry out a piece of business for them.

"That piece of business was to be the assassination

215

of Quebec's Premier. The NATO infrastructure had concluded that such a scheme would be entirely believable to Montenegro and his band because of the ill will between Quebec and the rest of Canada. Among terrorists throughout the world, the Quebec movement was viewed as a bourgeois struggle of no real political import; so Montenegro would have no second thoughts about carrying out the act.

"Montenegro actually thought it was an excellent idea and arranged for his top lieutenants to pick up the first shipment of arms in Toronto. That plane had been loaded with modern 111-3 automatic rifles and heat-detecting personal missiles.

"The NATO game plan called for the apprehension of Montenegro before the assassination, a news black-out, and the subsequent detonation of the plane over Lake Ontario with Montenegro's henchmen aboard.

"Because of policy directives and ineptitude, Montenegro slipped through the Mountie cordon and shot Lemoux, who had hurled himself between the Premier and the assassin. In the confusion that followed and because he had not relied on the escape route planned by his hosts, Montenegro escaped out of the country and returned to his headquarters in Libya.

"Montenegro's associates weren't as fortunate. Their plane took off as scheduled from Toronto under cover of the military. The Canadian government didn't dare risk capturing the terrorists because that would implicate them in the double-cross. It was much more efficient to detonate the plane over Lake Ontario. The government was equally determined to bury the story forever because it didn't want itself implicated in the assassination attempt, especially since it had gone sour.

"Kessler wrote the original story, figuring he'd be a Woodward or Bernstein. He took it to Pope, whose only interest in the end was to make a movie. Pope showed it to you and said he'd bought all the rights to the story, including the book rights. He made a deal with you that he'd write a second script, the King George assassination story, as a substitute if you'd come up with the money for the picture. You agreed to put up the money as long as the real story was destroyed.

"Pope had Kessler write the King George script allegedly to serve as a cover for investors. When Kessler realized he had been double-crossed and Pope was going to shoot the King George script instead of the real story, he got mad. But there was nothing he could· do. Pope owned all the rights. He could have spilled all his guts and the story to the media. He would have gotten some glory but not the kind of money he expected to make from a film and possible book on the Montenegro story. All his hard work was tied up in the contract with Pope. It rested on Pope's decision.

"You got scared at the last minute and decided that even the King George script was too close to the truth. So you started doing everything you could to stop the movie from being made. You were content just to use scare tactics at first. Everyone in the country knew about the Flock of God people. They provided you with an excellent cover. You knew every move we made because you had our phones tapped.

"You had Pope where you could control him, but Kessler was another story. When he showed up at Dunkin's party and started talking, your operatives were listening.

"When Dunkin walked Kessler to the cab downstairs, Kessler alluded to the ten thousand guns that you'd promised Montenegro. After the party broke up, Dunkin had some time to reflect on what Kessler had said. It hadn't made any sense at first, but the more he got to thinking about it, the more he decided Kessler just might have been trying to tell him something important.

"He called Pope, but Pope wouldn't admit anything, even after Dunkin started talking about the ten thousand guns. Instead Pope threw a fit and told Dunkin to mind his own business. He warned Dunkin not to tell anyone about what Kessler had said. Pope told him above all not to go around talking about such things over the telephone. But Dunkin couldn't let it lie. He called Bridges next because he knew Bridges and Pope had been in-

217

volved with Kessler from the beginning. But Bridges wouldn't have anything to do with him.

"Dunkin was beginning to get worried. That's when he started over to my place, stopping on the way to use a pay phone. Your operatives caught up with him right outside my hotel and shot him.

"Pope was getting worried over the original call and couldn't sleep. He knew once Kessler started talking they'd both be sitting pigeons. He called Dunkin back. The city police were already at his place and told him Dunkin was dead. Pope figured he was next.

"He grabbed Catherine out of bed, got her dressed, and took off in the middle of the night. He wouldn't tell her anything except that he was in great danger. She did the only thing she could and took him to the only truly safe place she knew in the city. The Reverend Smith's hideout.

"If you'd gotten hold of Pope first, the whole thing might have died a quiet death. But you didn't. I did."

"That's enough," he snapped finally.

"Are my five minutes up?" I asked him innocently.

"That's the most absurd story I've ever heard," he said. "I'll thank you to leave."

"Okay," I said, "but we're still going to make the movie. I came to you first because I thought you'd like to be among the first to know."

I got up and started for the door.

"Why do you think I should know?" he asked just as I reached the door.

I stopped, turned around, and came slowly back toward him.

"Because you were acting Minister of Defense during the attempted assassination," I told him. "Even if you weren't involved, you were responsible."

He looked at me and let out a deep sigh.

"Please sit down," he said.

I continued to stand. He got up from his desk and began to pace nervously as he spoke. He pointed to the manuscript.

"It's all in here?" he asked.

"Just the story part. The rest I ad-libbed."

"Where did you get it?"

"From Pope."

"Then he's alive."

"Yes, but I wouldn't worry about him. He's afraid of you," I told him. "But I'm not."

"I take it you haven't shown this to anyone else."

"Maybe, maybe not." I wanted to see how far I could string him along.

He sat down heavily in his chair.

"Some of what you say is true, unfortunately, Mr. Nevers. But you must believe me. I didn't know about it until afterward."

I didn't say anything.

"You also must understand," he continued, "that what happened was done to catch Montenegro. As you said, one of the most vicious criminals in modern history. The fact that we failed is something we all have to live with. Who knows when your relatives or you yourself will be on a plane that he hijacks or blows up."

I still said nothing.

"As for not making our actions public, surely you can understand why. We're a nation of twenty-four million split down the middle. When you are responsible for that many people, you must sometimes make decisions that aren't as neat and clean as you'd like them to be. But you still have to make them. Decisions, which in the long run, will be best for everyone."

"I don't know about your problems," I shot back. "All I know is that Danielle Davis, Clem Dunkin, and Harold D. Kessler are dead. They worked for me. They're my responsibility."

He stood up again, picked up the script and held it out to me.

"Mr. Nevers, be reasonable. If the truth came out, there would be bloodshed and fighting in the streets. We'd risk civil war."

"And you'd probably hang."

"No." He shook his head and tried a little smile on me, then thought better of it. "Nothing will happen to

219

me because I don't believe you'll make this movie. If you're reasonable, I'm sure there will be more money available from the government to make other films."

"Are you trying to offer me a bribe?" I asked.

It was his turn to look at me coldly.

"If you're smart, you'll listen. As I said, the government has the responsibility for twenty-four million. It cannot let a few sacrifice that for their own selfish interests."

"You had Dani, Clem, and Kessler killed, didn't you? And you would have killed Pope if you'd gotten your hands on him. And you'd probably have me killed if I walk out that door."

"In politics there are choices, and not always between good and evil. Sometimes it's a choice between bad and worse, sometimes between good and better. It's the long term and the majority that in the end must profit."

"The trouble with you, Mr. Minister, is that you want most to be making those choices. Making good or bad ones is a poor second on your list of priorities."

I turned to leave again.

"Wait." He called me back.

"No," I said. "Your time's run out."

I opened the door wide. Pierre Lemoux was just on the other side in his wheelchair. He had a copy of the movie script in his lap. He wheeled himself into Devoir's office and was followed by a mob of reporters, camera crews, and soundmen from all the papers and stations, who had all been given copies of the original script.

Chapter Forty-Two

In the end there were no riots. The people of the nation showed the most restraint, perhaps with just the slightest edge of cynical resignation. It wasn't the first scandal to come out of high places and it wouldn't be the last. As for the French-English factor, it was Lemoux himself who rose to the occasion and called for an end to the hate that could have caused such a thing to happen.

The government for its own part did a masterful job of sidestepping the issue and forming a Royal Commission to investigate the incident. In fact, they were so successful that they managed to survive another non-confidence vote and remain in power for a few more months until the opposition could collect enough of the separatist votes across the country into a unified front. Pierre Lemoux became the first separatist Prime Minister of the country. Ironically once the separatist elements got into power, they lost their appetite for separation, at least for the time being. But that's another story.

Before the government fell, Devoir was forced to resign, although he never admitted any wrongdoing. And although he claimed no knowledge of the Montenegro incident, he did admit responsibility. It was generally accepted that he also knew and directed the operations. To save face after his resignation, the government appointed him Ambassador to Jamaica. Two days after he arrived, he was gunned down in the men's room of a Kingston movie theater. The gunmen were never caught, but Montenegro claimed credit for the assassination as revenge for the double-cross and the murder of his men.

The real story did get made into a movie. Bridges used the publicity to embarrass Farrell King to take the part of the Canadian army officer who had secretly infiltrated Montenegro's operation. Catherine played the go-between for the Canadians and the womanizer Montenegro. She was sensational.

The movie was a box office smash, and everyone who had invested made money. Bridges and the Mosconis formed their own company and they went on to make three more pictures together. The film venture also gave the government its first opportunity to pry into the Mosconi empire and bleed them for millions in back taxes.

The success of the movie attracted a lot more production to the country, and O'Shea was forced to open the ranks of his organization to more people. Independents who wanted to do pictures outside the union structure were permitted, but they had to meet certain minimum pay scales.

The Flock of God sect surfaced again to face the bail-jumping charges. Backed up by Catherine's money and a promise to lead a peaceful existence, they were given suspended sentences, since the original charges against them had been minor. There was good reason to believe that they had, in fact, dynamited my plant at Ajax but that was never proved. The insurance company wrote it off. As for the fire at Kleinberg and the murders of Dani and Dunkin, it was pretty certain they had been carried out through some network within the power structure with links to Devoir, but that was never proven either.

One little item of curiosity did surface. When we were trying to figure out who had sent the nude pictures of Catherine to the Reverend Smith in the beginning, a very embarrassed Catherine admitted that she had sent them.

"I don't really know why," she insisted. "I guess after all those years, I just wanted my father to pay some attention to me."

Pope settled down. Once he had a solid picture

under his belt again, he started getting more offers. He even had an offer to do the King George assassination story. He turned it down because he thought he'd be repeating himself, but he sold the property for a half million dollars and ten points on the producer's gross receipts. He shared the money with all the original participants. He and Catherine were finally married. I stood in as best man. The Reverend Davidson Smith officiated, although he admitted he still didn't approve of Catherine's life-style or her husband.

Finally, the plant at Ajax started producing tomatoes and lettuce and began paying for itself. With that and the money from the movies, I had enough to pay my taxes, my debts, clear my obligations with the Mosconis, and still have enough left over for another grab at the big brass ring. I should have been a lot happier. But somehow I wasn't because the one person who should have been there to share it all with me wasn't.

If there was any way I could have, I would have traded all the nice things for one more day with Dani. No one ever smiled in the right places like she did.